Further Adventures of a Country Doctor

A. J. CRONIN

Original publication dates:

"Surgeon Without a Knife"
Hearst's International / Cosmopolitan magazine, August 1936

"Delirium Cordis"
Hearst's International / Cosmopolitan magazine, April 1937

"Better Than Medicine"
Hearst's International / Cosmopolitan magazine, June 1937

"What Money *Can't* Buy"
Hearst's International / Cosmopolitan magazine, July 1937

"Profit and Loss"
Hearst's International / Cosmopolitan magazine, February 1938

"No Imagination"
Hearst's International / Cosmopolitan magazine, June 1938

"Conduct Unbecoming"
Hearst's International / Cosmopolitan magazine, July 1938

"Judgment of the Gods"
Hearst's International / Cosmopolitan magazine, August 1938

"The Man Who Came Back"
Hearst's International / Cosmopolitan magazine, September 1938

"Inheritance"
Hearst's International / Cosmopolitan magazine, April 1939

"Night Call"
Hearst's International / Cosmopolitan magazine, June 1939

"The Third Ingredient"
Hearst's International / Cosmopolitan magazine, July 1939

Copyright © 1936, 1937, 1938, 1939 A. J. Cronin

ISBN: 978-1543289190

A. J. Cornell Publications

CONTENTS

Surgeon Without a Knife	4
Delirium Cordis	14
Better Than Medicine	26
What Money *Can't* Buy	37
Profit and Loss	50
No Imagination	61
Conduct Unbecoming	72
Judgment of the Gods	83
The Man Who Came Back	94
Inheritance	105
Night Call	118
The Third Ingredient	126

SURGEON WITHOUT A KNIFE

OFTEN, WHEN young Doctor Finlay Hyslop felt in need of exercise after a long day's driving in the gig, he would walk in the evening to the Lea Brae. It was a favorite walk, approached from Levenford by a gentle incline and sweeping steeply westward to the firth. From the top the view was superb. On a still summer evening, with the sun sinking behind Ardfillan hills, the wide water of the estuary below and the faint haze of a steamer's smoke mellowing the far horizon, it was a place to stir the soul. Yet for Finlay Hyslop it was ruined by Sam Forrest and his wheeled chair.

Up Sam would come, red-faced, bulging with fat, lying back on the cushions like a lord, with poor Peter Lennie panting and pushing the chair. Then at the top, while Peter gasped and wiped the sweat from his brow, Sam would majestically relinquish the little metal steering rod, pull a plug from his pocket, bite enormously and, mouthing his quid like a great big ox, gaze solemnly, not at the view but at the steep hill beneath as though to say: "Here, my friends—here was the place where the awful thing happened!"

It all went back a matter of five long years.

Then Peter Lennie was a spry young fellow of twenty-seven, very modest and obliging, proprietor of the small general store in College Street which he had named Lennie's Emporium. In fiction the convention exists that meek little men have large domineering wives, but in reality it is seldom so. And Retta Lennie was as small, slight and unassertive as her husband. In consequence, in business they were often "put upon." But for all that, things went pretty well, the future was opening out nicely, and they lived comfortably with their two children in a semidetached house out Barloan way, a genteel quarter to which Levenford tradesmen aspire.

Now, in Peter Lennie, the humble little counter-jumping tradesman, there lurked unsuspected longings for adventure. There were moments when, lying reflectively in bed with Retta of a Sunday morning, he would stare at the ceiling and suddenly declare: "India!" (Or it might be "China!") "There's a place we ought to see some day!"

Perhaps it was this romantic boldness which led to the purchase of the tandem bicycle, for though at that moment the craze for "a bicycle built for two" was at its height, in the ordinary way Peter would never have done anything so rash. But buy the tandem he did—a shining instrument of motion, a wicked, pneumatic-tired machine which cost a mint of good money and which, being uncrated, caused Retta to gasp incredulously:

"Oh, Peter!"

"Get about on it," he remarked, trying to speak nonchalantly. "See places. Easy!"

It was, however, not quite so easy. There was, for instance, the difficulty about Retta's bloomers. She was a modest little woman, was Retta, and it cost Peter a week of solid argument and persuasion before he could coax his wife into the light of day in this fashionable but apparently improper garment.

Then Peter and Retta set out to master the machine. They practiced shyly, toward dusk, in the quiet lanes around Barloan, and they fell off quite a lot. Oh, it was great fun! Retta, in her bloomers, was extremely fetching. Peter liked to lift her up as, red-cheeked and giggling, she sprawled gracefully in the dust. They had their courtship all over again. And when, finally, defying all laws of gravitation, they spun round Barloan Toll without a single wobble, they agreed that never before had life been so thrilling for them both.

Peter, significantly producing a newly purchased road map, decided that on Sunday they would have their first real run.

It dawned fine, that Sunday; the sky was open and the roads were dry. They set off, Peter bowed dauntlessly over the front handlebars, Retta manfully pedaling behind. They bowled down the High Street conscious of admiring, yes, even envious stares. *Ting-a-ling-ting-ting* went their little bell. A great moment. *Ting-a-ling-ting-ting!*

They swung left—steady, Retta, steady—over the bridge; put their backs into the Knoxhill ascent; then dipped over the crest of the Lea Brae. Down the brae they went, faster, faster. The wind whistled past them. Never had flight been swifter than this. It was great, it was glorious, but heavens, it was awfully quick; far, far quicker than either had bargained for.

From a momentary exaltation Retta turned pale. "Brake, Peter, brake!" she shrieked.

Nervously he jammed on the brakes, the tandem shuddered, and Retta nearly went over his head. At that he lost his wits completely, loosed the brake altogether and tried to get his feet out of the pedal clips. The machine took the bit between its teeth and shot down the hill like a rocket gone mad.

At the foot of the brae was Sam Forrest. Sam had been down looking for drift on the Lea shore—that, indeed, was one of Sam's two occupations, the other being to support with great industry the corner of the Fitter's Arms. Actually, Sam was so seldom away from the Fitter's Arms that it never was in any real danger of falling down. In plain words, Sam was a loafer, a big, fat, boozy ne'er-do-well with a wife who did washing and a houseful of clamorous children who did not.

Sam, with an air at once fascinated and bemused, watched the bicycle approach. It came so quickly he wondered for a second if he were seeing right. Saturday, the night before, had been a heavy night for Sam, and his brain was still slightly fuddled. Down ... down ... down whizzed the tandem.

Peter, with a face frozen to horror, made a last effort at control. The machine collided with the curb, shot across the road and crashed straight into Sam. In point of fact, it hit him fair in the back as he turned to run. There was a desperate roar from Sam, a loud clatter as the pieces of the machine dispersed themselves, followed by a long silence. Then Retta and Peter picked themselves out of the ditch.

Peter grinned feebly at Retta, and Retta, who felt like fainting, smiled weakly in return. But suddenly they recollected. What about Sam? Ah, poor Sam lay groaning in the dust. They rushed over to him.

"Are you hurt?" cried Peter.

"I'm dead," he moaned. "Ye've killed me, ye bloody murderers!"

Terrible silence, punctuated by Sam's groans. Nervously Peter tried to raise the fallen man, who was quite double his weight.

"Let me be! Let me be!" Sam roared. "You're tearin' me to bits."

Retta went whiter than ever. "Get up, Sam, do!" she implored. She knew him well, having refused him credit the week before.

But Sam wouldn't get up. The slightest attempt to raise him sent him into the most terrible convulsions, and his big beefy legs seemed now no more able to support him than watery blancmange.

By this time Retta and Peter were at their wits' end: they saw Sam a mutilated corpse and themselves standing palely in the dock while the judge sternly assumed the black cap. However, at this moment help arrived in the shape of Rafferty's light lorry. Rafferty, the butter-and-egg man, had been down at Ardfillan collecting eggs. With his help Sam was hoisted up among the eggs and driven to his house in the Vennel. A few eggs were smashed in the process but Peter and Retta didn't mind. They would pay, they protested passionately; oh, yes, they would pay. Nothing mattered so long as Sam got safely back.

At last Sam was home and in his bed surrounded by his curious progeny, sustained by the shrill lamentations of his wife.

"The doctor," she whined. "We'll need the doctor."

"Ye-yes, yes," stammered Peter. "I'll fetch the doctor." What had he been thinking of? Of course they must have the doctor! He tore down the steps and ran.

At that time Doctor Snoddy lived in High Street adjacent to the Vennel. And it was Snoddy who came to Sam.

Sam lay on his back with his mouth open and his eyes closed. No martyr suffered more than did Sam during the examination.

The doctor, while puzzled, was impressed by Sam's condition—no bones broken, no internal injuries that he could find, but something seemingly wrong for all that, the patient's agony was so manifest. Snoddy was a small, prosy, pompous man with a tremendous sense of his own dignity, and finally, with a great show of professional knowledge, he made the ominous pronouncement: "It's the spine!"

Sam echoed the words with a hollow groan, and horror thrilled through to Peter's marrow.

"Ye understand," he whispered, "it was us to blame. We take full responsibility. He's to have everything that's needed. Nothing's too good for him. Nothing!"

That was the beginning. Nourishment was necessary for the invalid, good strong nourishment. Nourishment was provided. Stimulant. Peter saw that the brandy was the very best. A proper bed. Towels, linen, saucepans, jellies, tea, nightshirts, sugar, they all flowed gently to the sick man's home.

Later, some tobacco—to soothe the anguished nerves. And a little money, too, since Mrs. Forrest, tied to Sam's bedside, could not do her washing as before. "Run round with this to Sam's" became the order of the day. Snoddy, of course, was calling regular as the clock.

And finally there came the day when, taking Peter aside, he articulated the fatal word *paralysis!* Sam's life was saved; but Sam would never use his legs again.

"N-never?" Peter faltered. "I don't understand."

Snoddy laughed his pompous little laugh. "Just watch the poor fellow try to walk—then ye'll understand."

It was a staggering blow for Peter and Retta. They talked it over late into the night—over and over and over. But there was no way out. They had done it, they alone must foot the bill, and Sam—of course Sam, poor soul, his lot was far, far worse than theirs.

A Bath chair was bought—Peter sweated when he saw the price—and Sam and his chair assumed their place in Levenford society. On the level his eldest son, aged fourteen, could wheel him easily and "down to the Emporium" became a favorite excursion of Sam's. He would sit outside the shop basking in the sun, sending in for tobacco or a pie. Now there was no talk of refusing him credit. Sam's credit was unlimited, and he had his weekly dole from Peter as well.

When the nine days' wonder of the wheeled chair subsided, Levenford forgot. Hardly anyone noticed it when Peter and Retta relinquished the cozy little Barloan house and moved into the rooms above the shop; when the little girl gave up her music lessons and the boy suddenly left the academy to earn a wage in Gillespie's office. The gray creeping into Peter's hair and the worried frown on Retta's brow evoked little interest and less sympathy. As Sam himself put it, with a pathetic shake of his head: "They have their legs, at any rate!"

This was indeed the very phrase which Sam employed to Doctor Hyslop on that fateful summer evening of early July.

It was a fine bright evening, with the view looking

its very best. The doctor stood on the brae trying to find tranquility in the sight. Tonight his surgery had worried him, the day had been troublesome, and his mood was cantankerous. At length the quiet of the scene sank into him. And then over the crest of the brae came Sam in the wheeled chair.

Hyslop swore. The history of Sam and Peter had long been known to him, and the sight of the big bloated fellow fastened like a parasite on the lean and hungry Lennie goaded him immeasurably. He watched them draw near irritably, observing Peter's physical distress and, as they reached the summit, he made a caustic comment on the difficulties of propelling inert matter uphill.

"He canna complain," sighed Sam. "He has his legs, at any rate."

And then, instinctively, Hyslop looked at Sam's legs as they lay snugly in the long wheeled chair. They were, strangely, a remarkably stout pair of legs. Fat, like the rest of Sam, bulging Sam's blue serge trousers. Peculiar, thought the doctor, that there should be no atrophy, no wasting of these ineffectual limbs!

He stared and stared at Sam's legs with a growing penetration; then with a terrible intentness he stared at the smug-faced Sam. Supposing—supposing all these years . . .

And suddenly, as he stood beside the wheeled chair on the edge of the brae, suddenly with a devilish impulse he took the flat of his boot and gave the chair a frightful push. Without a word of warning it shot off downhill.

Peter stood gaping at the bolting chair like a man petrified by the repetition of dreadful history; then he let out a nervous scream.

Sam, roaring like a bull, was trying to control the chair. But the chair had no brakes. It careened all over the road, dashed at a frantic speed into the hedge, overturned and shot Sam bang into a bed of nettles.

For two seconds Sam was lost to view in the green sea of the stinging nettles; then, miraculously, he arose.

Cursing with rage, he scrambled to his feet and ran up to Hyslop. "What the hell," he shouted, brandishing his fists—"what the hell did ye do that for?"

"To see if ye could walk!" Hyslop shouted back, and hit Sam first.

Peter and Retta have returned to the Barloan house. The wheeled chair is sold, and Sam is back at his old job: supporting the corner of the Fitter's Arms.

But every time Finlay Hyslop drives past, Sam curses and spits upon the ground.

DELIRIUM CORDIS

THIS IS not a festive story! It is, indeed, no story at all, but truth, grim, merciless truth beginning with an attack of d.t.'s and ending—well, you shall see how it ends.

It is about a man whom Doctor Finlay Hyslop loved, a man by the name of Muir—David Muir—Master of Arts of St. Andrews University—scholar, poet, drunkard, failure, fool . . .

"Jeannie Lee wants yet doctor."

"What for?"

"It's Drucken Davie, doctor."

"And who in the name of wonder is Drucken Davie?"

"Oh, he's—he's just Drucken Davie, doctor."

"And what's like the matter with Drucken Davie, then?"

"Oh, he's just drunk again, doctor!"

Hyslop gazed reflectively at the dirty little boy who had brought this message from the Quay Side slum where Jeannie Lee let out lodgings to the submerged of Levenford. Then he said gruffly, "If he's just drunk, he doesn't need a doctor."

"But he's no' just ordinar' drunk," came the knowing answer. "Blind drunk or dead drunk, that's nothing out o' the way for Davie. But this time he's got the d.t.'s as weel."

So Hyslop, with an ill grace, trudged down to Jeannie Lee's lodging-house, which was the worst infamy in that infamous nest of Quay Side slums. He hammered on the blistered door and was at last admitted by a young slattern in a shawl.

"Jeannie Lee's had to go out," she announced, fixing the doctor with her fine bold eyes. "She says she'll no' be responsible for your fee. She says to tell ye Davie Muir'll pay ye when he's better. She says—"

Hyslop cut her short. "Never mind what she says. Let me see your Davie and get out of here."

"All right, all right. Keep your hair on. There's his room—up there!"

It was a small room at the back of the house, so dark that the doctor had to stand still until his eyes readjusted themselves to the gloom. Then he made out Davie Muir lying on a truckle bed.

Davie still wore his clothes and his boots. He was unshaven, his coat daubed with mud, his collar torn at the neck, his eyes staring with a sort of horror into infinity. Around him lay the evidence of poverty, wretchedness, misery: a bare table, an old trunk, some empty bottles and a score of battered books.

"What a mess!" muttered Hyslop involuntarily.

The sound roused Davie. He sprang to a sitting position and burst into a torrent of speech. His face purpled, the veins of his neck thickened until they stood like cords. He had the dreadful look of a soul tortured in the forgotten depths of hell. He raved on. There is no purpose in recording the painful rhetoric of imagination driven mad by alcohol. But as the spasm passed and he fell back on the bed, he quoted suddenly:

*"Scilicet occidimus, nec spes est ulla salutis,
Dumque loquor, vultus obruit unda meos . . ."*

The manner in which the lines were spoken, the sudden contrast with besotted ranting, arrested Hyslop: shook him from his instinctive desire to be out of the fetid room as soon as he could jab a hypodermic of morphine into the sick man's arm. Instead, he stayed an hour, watching Davie Muir until he fell into troubled sleep, trying to pierce beneath the beard and grime which encrusted him, endeavoring to visualize, to recreate his youth. Not that Davie looked old—not more than thirty-five was Hyslop's estimate. His hair was still thick and dark, his brow fine, his features not yet blurred: but there lay upon him an ageless experience.

Before he left Hyslop tidied the room as best he

could. He picked up a book; it was the *Aeneid;* another, *Paolo & Francesca;* another, one of the bawdiest de Goncourt novels. Hyslop sighed. Then he stepped out of the room.

That night he questioned Cameron—discreetly—for Cameron would never be drawn if he scented gossip in the wind.

"So ye've seen Drucken Davie," Cameron ruminated, between puffs of his pipe. "Well! Well! There's a tale ye wouldn't credit if ye saw it in broad print." A pause. "Poor Davie Muir! To look at him now ye wouldn't believe he was once the star prizeman of his year at St. Andrews. He knew Latin and Greek as I know broad Scots. They prophesied a' things for him from a professorship at Oxford to a seat on the Woolsack itself. And what is he now? A half-time contributor to the *Advertiser!*

"Five years ago he came to Levenford as classics master at the academy. And for a couple of years he held the post. But he lost it in the end. Faugh! I cannot bear to think on it, I'm so sorry for the poor deevil. I cannot be bothered telling you any more the now."

"Is it a long story, then?" Hyslop inquired.

"No," said Cameron briefly. "It's a short story. Damned short. One solitary word. Drink! Good night to ye." And Cameron went off to bed.

Next morning Hyslop went to see Davie again, and on several mornings after that. Something drew him to Davie Muir, perhaps the helplessness, the rare, pathetic charm of the man himself.

THERE WAS no doubt of Davie's charm. Scholarly, sensitive, persuasive, witty—he was delightful company. Little by little Hyslop came to like Davie Muir, to admire him, and then to love him. And so it happened one afternoon, when Davie was almost fully recovered and able to stagger shakily to his legs, that Hyslop braced himself to take the plunge.

"Davie," he blurted out, "why don't you keep off the drink? I'll do everything I can to help you."

Davie gave a short laugh. With the first touch of bitterness he had displayed, he declared, "The Hyslop treatment, eh? You drop something in my tea when I'm not looking. Tasteless. Odorless. And I'm cured the morn's morning. It's a marvelous suggestion, if only for its novelty!"

Hyslop colored. "I was just thinking—"

"It's no good thinking, lad," interposed Davie in a softer voice. "And it's no good doing, either. Don't you think I've tried before? I've had a dozen doctors—Edinburgh, London, ay, Berlin too. I've been in sanatoria till I'm sick of them. I've tried everything. But it's no use. The thing's ingrained in me. It *is* me. I'm rotten with it. Rotten, I tell you." His voice rose as he went on. "I'm a drunkard, a habitual confirmed drunkard. The minute I'm able to leave this house I'll go round to Pat Marney's pub. I entertain the boys. When I'm half tight I tell them bawdy stories from the French. When I'm whole tight I convulse them with Greek epigrams. They like me there and I like them. When I'm drunk, ye understand. At any rate, that's where I'll go the minute you leave me. I'll sit there and booze every penny I've got. With luck, I'll last six months, till I get another go of d.t.'s."

A heavy silence fell. Then Hyslop said, "If that's the way of it, Davie, I suppose there's nothing more to be said or done." And he went out of the room.

It happened, of course, exactly as Davie had predicted. The hospitable doors of Marney's pub swung open an hour later, and Davie Muir walked in.

The evening wore on. The Yard emptied. All the "boys" rolled in, riveters, fitters, laborers—all glad to see "our Davie" back. The drink percolated softly, generously through Davie's starved tissues. He glowed. He set them guffawing. And at closing time, he went home and fell dead drunk upon his bed.

Next morning was fine. He rose late and went down to Marney's for a stiffener. Along Quay Side a brisk breeze held; the sky was blue; the sun shone warmly. It was a day to move the heart.

As he sidled round the corner of the quay, Davie heard someone hail him. It was Kate Marney, Pat's fat wife, all dressed up. With pride in her voice she observed, "Would you pass me like that now, Mr. Muir, and me out walkin' wid me daughter Rosie home from school?"

"Sorry, Mrs. Marney," Davie said thickly. The light hurt his eyes. He felt intolerably ill, dying for a drink. He vaguely remembered hearing of Pat's daughter, his only daughter Rosie, who had been sent away from the pub to a convent school. He turned to look at her. His gaze absorbed her clear young beauty. Then his eyes fell abjectly.

"Lovely morning for a walk," he muttered. "Sorry! Got to keep an appointment." He walked swiftly away, making straight for the pub.

He drank a chaser slowly, listening to Pat, who was full of the return of his daughter.

"Turned seventeen, she is, Davie me boy, but innocent as a chile. Didn't ye see her as ye come by? Faith, she's lovelier nor a flower."

"She is lovely," Davie repeated in a low voice. "Lovelier than a rose." And he murmured, " 'Hither all dewy from her convent fetched . . .' "

Pat beamed. "And very appropr'ate them words is too. Much appreciated by her dad. Same again, me boy? Have it on the house for the occasion."

"Later, Pat. Later. Not just now."

Davie walked out, trying to think. He crossed the road, took up his stand on the opposite pavement. In an hour's time Rose and her mother returned. The girl saw him, gave him a fleeting smile of recognition; then she was gone. His heart resumed its beating. "Why am I not dead?" he groaned to himself.

He went home to his lodging. It had happened to him at last. He was in love. She was sweet, innocent, lovely and seventeen. He was thirty-four and a drunkard. He sat for a long time. Thinking, thinking. The filth and squalor of his room infuriated him. He rose up, kicking over his chair. Suddenly he cried out in a frenzy of determination:

"Why shouldn't I? I can do it if I want to. I've never wanted to before! But now I do!"

He seized his hat and almost ran to Arden House. He burst into Hyslop's surgery. "Doctor," he exclaimed, "I'm going to do it! I'm cutting out the drink. For good this time, you understand. Will you help me as you said?"

Levenford, of course, smiled up its sleeve when Davie appeared all spruced up and shaved, in a suit of Hyslop's. Levenford was highly amused when he changed his lodging from the squalid Quay Side room to a decent apartment in Church Street. Levenford had a finger on its nose when, at Hyslop's importuning, Jackson of the *Advertiser* gave Davie a full-time job on the staff at thirty shillings a week. Levenford knew all this wouldn't last. Levenford waited.

It seemed, however, as if Levenford might wait in vain. Davie led the quietest existence possible, doing his work by day, remaining in his room at night. Few guessed that his composure was merely outward. Within, Davie Muir drained the cup of suffering to the bitter, bitter dregs. He knew the agony of maddening sleepless nights. But he held grimly on, clinging to his hope, his inspiration. And Hyslop stood by him, helping him as a doctor, as a friend. It looked, in fact, as though Davie would at last win through.

SUMMER CAME, a soft early summer which still

held the freshness of spring. And in the fine evenings Davie, feeling stronger and safer now, would stroll from the town toward the road that led to the Winton Hills.

It was a pleasant walk, but it was not the beauty of the spot which drew Davie there. He came because it was Rose Marney's favorite walk. His intention was not to intercept her. He was still far too diffident, too humble, too full of the consciousness of his own defects. He wanted merely to see her in the distance as a man upon earth might vision the beauty of a star. His love for her was spiritual, idealized. Her far-off presence sang to him—a song of innocence. But one evening, as was inevitable, they met on the edge of the moorland.

As Rose approached, Davie's heart beat painfully, deliriously. He felt that she would never recollect him; but she smiled and stopped. They spoke, looked at the view together. Then he accompanied her down the road. It was all perfectly innocent and natural.

Davie exerted himself to be interesting, amusing, gay. With a sudden uplift of joy he saw that she was enjoying herself immensely. Then at the foot of the road he halted. "I'll let you go on now," he said. "That's to say, if you don't mind."

She stared at him in surprise. "But aren't you coming into town, too?"

He would have given his head to have walked home through the town with her. But he was wiser than she.

"No," he declared cheerfully. "I've got to see someone at Darroch—for the *Advertiser*, you know. I'll walk round the back way."

He did actually in sheer exuberance walk to Darroch, treading upon air. He might—alas!—have saved himself the journey. He had been seen talking to Rose, seen by Dougal Todd. That great-hearted citizen of Levenford flew as fast as his flat sanctimonious feet could carry him to spread the news that young Rose Marney had been seen on a lonely country road with Davie Muir.

The scandal reached Pat Marney on the following day. His fat, good-natured face congested with rage. He grabbed his stick and set out to find Davie. They met in the crowded High Street.

"You dog," shouted Marney, "you drunken dog! You think you'd come round me daughter like you do your woman in Quay Street. You that sat swilling me drink! You sponging, drunken waster! To think you'd dare touch my daughter." And he set upon Davie with his blackthorn like a man possessed.

Davie had no chance under that furious attack. He took a dozen violent blows on his head and shoulders before he was knocked senseless into the gutter.

He was unconscious for a long time, but came round at last to find half a dozen of his friends supporting him.

"Here, Davie, take this." A gill bottle was at Davie's lips and a gush of neat spirit was in his mouth. Instinctively he drank, drank thirstily. He was wounded, hurt, trembling. The whisky flowed into him like divine, long-forgotten fire.

"That's better," said a voice. "That's done you good, Davie. Come away and take a seat in the Fitter's Bar."

It was just across the road, the Fitter's Bar. They led him in there with great solicitude. Another drink was forced on him there. He couldn't resist. He drank feverishly. All his injured pride rose up, choking him. To think that Marney had struck him—him—David Muir, graduate with honors of St. Andrews! He would show Marney, and show him soon.

At six o'clock he left the Fitter's Bar accompanied by some others and made straight for Marney's pub. He burst in. Swaying drunkenly, he addressed himself to Pat behind the bar.

"You would strike a gentleman!" he shouted. "You filthy specimen of the genus hog Hibernia. And for what did you strike me? Simply because I, David Muir, did your blowzy female brat the honor of speaking to her."

He let out a loud besotted laugh. But he stopped laughing all at once. Rose stood at the open doorway leading to the Marney house. Horror and disgust were in her eyes. She had heard every word.

He looked at her stupidly, still oscillating gently upon his feet. There she was, his lovely Rose, his song of innocence. And he had called her a blowzy brat! His face went the color of clay. He let out a wild cry of mingled agony and despair. Then he staggered from the room.

For three whole days nothing was heard of Davie. But on the afternoon of the third day, at high tide in the river Leven, some children found something bobbing gently against the steps of Quay Side opposite the lodging house. It was the body of Davie Muir.

"Scilicet occidimus, nec spes est ulla salutis . . ."

To Finlay Hyslop and to Jackson of the *Advertiser* fell the melancholy duty of going through Davie's effects. There was nothing of value or importance. But in his room in High Street they found some verses written in Greek. Hyslop knew little of this language; yet he knew enough to see that they were odes written to Rose. He concealed them quickly.

As they came down the stairs, Jackson said, "I suppose the poor devil drowned himself in a fit of delirium tremens."

Hyslop was silent for a moment; then he shook his head sadly. "No, not that, Jackson. It was delirium—not of the head but of the heart. If you must give it a name, call it *delirium cordis!*"

BETTER THAN MEDICINE

FOLLOWING THE case of one Jeannie Hendry, who died tragically from scarlet fever at Shawhead Farm, the strained relations which had always existed between Hyslop and Cameron on the one side and Doctor Snoddie on the other developed into a positive feud.

Snoddie had a mean and spiteful nature; he was not the man either to forget or to forgive, and in the months which followed it became increasingly clear that he was out to get his own back. In his official capacity of medical officer of health he did everything possible to annoy and harass Finlay Hyslop and Cameron in their work, but beyond everything, in his own practice he waged constant war by his efforts to "steal" a patient from his rivals on every opportunity.

"Hang it all," declared Hyslop heatedly to Cameron after such an effort of Snoddie's had almost succeeded, "this is going beyond words. The man's making a dead-set at our best patients. Bah! I've no use for him whatever."

Which shows, as, indeed, this story will shortly prove, that Hyslop had momentarily forgotten the well-known axiom that in this world there is a use for everything!

It was winter, and the weather was abominable. It had snowed and rained, snowed again, then rained on top of that, until the roads were almost impassable. Wicked going and weary work it made for Cameron and his young partner. Pleurisy and pneumonia ravaged the countryside. It was the worst time of all the year, when to work a scattered practice was little better than slavery in its crudest form.

Late one night Hyslop stamped into the dining room after a killing day and sank into a chair. With a sigh of relief he relaxed before the fire, then accepted a bowl of steaming broth from Janet.

Outside, the wind howled in the darkness, battering hailstones against the windowpanes like a fusillade of icy shot.

Half an hour later Cameron came in, equally worn out, his gaunt, weather-beaten features pinched with cold and fatigue. He came forward slowly and stretched out his hands to the fire, while the steam rose from his damp clothing.

A silence of sympathetic understanding linked the two men: the knowledge of common endeavor, of work done in the face of hardship.

Then Cameron, with a long expiration of his

breath, went to the sideboard, poured out some whisky, added a little sugar, then marched to the fireplace and picked up the kettle which always sang there. But just as he gratefully raised the steaming brew to his lips the phone bell rang.

"Damn!" he muttered. He lowered the toddy untouched, and Hyslop stared at him in dismay.

Two minutes of waiting; then Janet came in.

"It's from Mr. Currie of Langloan," she said to Cameron. "They've been expecting you all day long." Pause. "And now they want to know if you're coming at all!" Crossing her arms upon her bosom, Janet gazed at the old doctor like a schoolmistress sorely put out by a favorite pupil.

Cameron groaned. "The de'il dang me for an eediot! What was I thinking o' to forget Neil Currie? And me passing his very door twice."

Hyslop was silent. He well knew the misery of missing a call in the rush of the day's work and having to retrace weary steps. Quickly he rose to make the call for Cameron, when Janet spoke again.

"It's no use your goin', Doctor Hyslop. They're fair upset at Langloan. They say if you're not up yourself, Doctor Cameron, within half an hour, they'll have to fetch Doctor Snoddie instead."

At this information Cameron's lined face took on a deeper shade. "Dang my bones!" he exclaimed, "Did ye ever hear the like of that?" He put down the toddy untasted and buttoned up his coat.

"Let me go," protested Hyslop. "You're dead-beat."

"Dead-beat or no," said Cameron, "I'm going. Neil Currle'll never be satisfied unless I show face myself. Confound it, Hyslop, we're taking no more risks to let that Snoddie in."

"I'll send for Jamie and the gig," said Janet.

"No." growled Cameron. "Jamie's worn out, and the beast's half foundered. It isn't far to Langloan. I'll walk."

In spite of Hyslop's attempts to dissuade him, the old doctor had his way.

NEIL CURRIE was one of his oldest friends, an important man in the burgh, and at present laid low by a bad attack of pleurisy. Failing to visit such a patient might be construed as neglect. If through this Cameron were ousted from the case, what a feather it would be in Snoddie's cap!

That, more than anything, weighed with Cameron. Turning up his coat collar, he braced himself against the wind.

But Hyslop was uneasy. He sat listening to the gale outside, seeing Cameron plodding through the slush.

When Cameron returned an hour later, he was completely exhausted. Nevertheless, he wheezed triumphantly: "I've smoothed out that affair. I explained to Neil how it happened. Everything's right as rain between us. He's got a bad patch of pleurisy, mind ye. For heaven's sake, don't let me forget to see him in the morning."

He sat down wearily and peered into the fire; he coughed sharply, then went on with a painful chuckle, "They were on the point of sendin' for Snoddie when I arrived. But I put a spoke in his wheel, I tell ye." He slumped back limply in his chair.

Hyslop was now thoroughly concerned. He left the room and asked the housekeeper to bring some hot soup. But when Janet brought it, Cameron refused it, and a moment later, he said to Hyslop:

"I think I'll get upstairs." He rose, but halfway to the door he pressed his hand to his side and collapsed.

Hyslop got Cameron upstairs to his bedroom, helped him into bed. He made a rapid examination and did not like the condition of Cameron's chest.

Ignoring the old man's protests, he poulticed him, dosed him with hot toddy and quinine. Cameron fell into a restless sleep.

Next morning, Hyslop found his patient feverish, breathing rapidly, tormented by a short, suppressed cough. Cameron had pneumonia, lobar pneumonia, and Cameron himself was aware of the fact, for he gasped:

"It seems I'm in for it this time."

Cameron was in for it with a vengeance. And confronted by this grave emergency, Hyslop marshaled all his forces to meet it. He telephoned Linklaters', the wholesale chemists in Glasgow who also ran a local medical agency. Through them he obtained a temporary assistant—a Highlander named Frazer, who arrived early that same afternoon.

Hyslop deputed to Frazer the surgeries and all the unimportant work; he himself rushed through the serious cases as quickly as he could. The rest of his time he devoted to Cameron.

Hyslop was well aware that there could be no miracle, no immediate cure. Lobar pneumonia ran nine days usually, before the crisis came, bringing relief. And so, with passionate intensity, he threw himself into the task of pulling Cameron through the nine fateful days.

Cameron, despite his pain and discomfort, was cheerful at the start. A nurse stood at the foot of the bed, ready to anticipate his every want. Everything was being done, and everything would be done, Hyslop thought grimly. He must pull Cameron through. He must!

In this fashion for the first three days all went smoothly, and the condition ran a normal course. But on the fourth day, with alarming unexpectedness, Cameron took a turn for the worse.

Hyslop redoubled his attentions. All that night and the following night he sat up with Cameron, making an almost superhuman effort to stem the ominous advancing tide. But without avail.

On the sixth day Cameron was definitely worse. On the seventh day, Hyslop had Hardman down from Glasgow.

Hardman, the best-known medical specialist in the west of Scotland, arrived in the afternoon. He was kind, but far from reassuring. He agreed with Hyslop's diagnosis and treatment, but Cameron, said he, was not so young as he had been. His strength had failed considerably, and he seemed now to offer little resistance to the malady.

In plain truth, Hardman held out little hope, and he could do no more than urge Hyslop to continue the measures which he was taking—to press the injections of strychnine; to resort to oxygen when necessary; but above everything, to try to stimulate the patient's powers to fight against the disease.

The eighth day came without a shadow of improvement. Though Hyslop doubled his efforts at stimulation, using strychnine, brandy and even oxygen; though he battled frantically to arrest the growing weakness in the sick man, it seemed as if all these things were useless. Cameron's old fighting quality seemed extinguished. He lay passive on his pillow.

By this time it had become known throughout Levenford how ill Cameron was. All day long messages and tokens of sympathy kept pouring into the house.

Then came the ninth day, pregnant with fatality.

All afternoon Hyslop sat watching Cameron's strength ebb away under his very eyes. Evening came—a still, cold evening, and with the falling darkness it seemed as if the mantle of death hung above the enfeebled figure in the bed. Cameron was conscious now, and almost placid.

"I'm afraid it's all up with me this time, lad," he

whispered.

Unable to reply, Hyslop shook his head violently. But Cameron went on.

"I'm glad to leave the practice to ye. It's in fair good shape. Ye'll do well wit' it—ay, maybe better than I've done" Come to that, I'd like ye to know, man, I've loved ye like a son."

The tears streamed from Hyslop's eyes; his body was shaken by sobs.

There was silence in the room for long time. Then, with a feeble glimmer of his old humor, Cameron screwed up his eyes and gazed at Hyslop.

"It's funny to think I got this goin' out to Currie's," he reflected. A pause for breath. "But mind ye, it was worth it, man. I'll go happy in the knowledge that I've done Snoddie in the e'e."

At these characteristic words, something flashed through Hyslop's brain. It was heaven-sent inspiration. Mastering his emotion, he looked at Cameron.

"That's the pity of it," he declared. "You didn't do Snoddie down, after all."

"What?" whispered Cameron. "What in thunder do ye mean?"

Hyslop shook his head. "No," he repeated, "that's the pity of it. The minute you were on your back, the Curries had Snoddie in. He's stolen them from us for good and all. 'Deed, he's bragging about it all over town."

A strange light began to glisten in Cameron's eyes. "D'ye mean to say," he muttered, "that Snoddie's bragging that he's licked me?"

"Indeed I do," replied Hyslop, concealing the hope which swelled within his breast.

Cameron gathered himself together. The light in the dim eyes grew; the old fighting spirit reawakened. "Is that a fact?" said he. "Here, hand me that bowl of gruel. I think I'll take a sup o't."

Trembling between exultation and anxiety, Hyslop took the bowl which Cameron had refused all day and spooned the gruel between the sick man's lips. When it was finished Cameron made an impatient gesture.

"It's fushionless stuff, that," he croaked. "Get me some strong beef tea."

He had his beef tea. Then he had his medicine, which previously he had fretfully waved away. Strength and determination seemed to flow back into him.

He spoke no more, but fell into a deep sleep. Waiting with grim intensity, Hyslop watched the sleeping man.

The minutes passed and merged into hours, then an apparently insignificant thing happened: beads of sweat broke on Cameron's brow. But to Hyslop it was not insignificant. He could have cried aloud. He felt Cameron's pulse, which was stronger and slower; took his temperature, which had fallen to normal.

It was the crisis. Cameron was saved!

Next morning Cameron woke up refreshed and bawling, albeit feebly, for nourishment. As he sipped some hough tea, all at once the bells of the town steeple began to peal.

"What's that?" asked Cameron. "Some eediot gettin' wed?"

"No," said Hyslop, "these bells are for you."

It was the truth. Jubilant at the news of Cameron's release from death, they were ringing the bells in thanksgiving. An overwhelming tribute to the respect in which the old doctor was held!

But there was no gratification in Cameron's heart, only a fierce determination. "Wait till I get hold of that Snoddie!" he muttered. "I'll give him bells."

Cameron's recovery was speedy. Three weeks later, he toddled downstairs.

THERE, IN the sitting room, he held a levee. All his friends called to congratulate him. Then, as the clock struck five, a man came in and advanced to shake hands. Hyslop hid a smile, for the man was Neil Currie.

"Weel!" cried Currie, pump-handling Cameron genially. "I'm delighted ye've cheated the de'il, like mysel'." Then, turning to pat Hyslop, "We owe a vote of thanks, you and me, to this young man. He's pulled the both o' us through."

Highly incensed, Cameron looked Currie up and down. "What in thunder are ye talking about?" he roared. "And by the same token, ye're no friend of mine. Didn't ye have Snoddie in the moment I was laid on my back?"

"Snoddie!" cried Currie, aghast. "What do you

mean, ye gomeril, and what do ye take me for? It was Hyslop here that saw me through from start to finish—in between the whiles he was nursing you."

Cameron's face was a study. "Weel, I'll be damned!" he said at last. Then, as understanding of the strategy which Hyslop had adopted dawned upon him, he laughed awkwardly, while a suspicious moisture crept into his eyes. "Weel," said he meekly, "Snoddie—I suppose, after all, the creature has his uses."

And so the last word was said upon it.

WHAT MONEY *CAN'T* BUY

THE LEGAL DEEDS admitting Finlay Hyslop to equal partnership with Doctor Cameron had been completed, and Hyslop, filled with real gratitude toward the testy but warmhearted old doctor, faced the future with a sense of his own good fortune and the firm determination to give of his very best.

Often, in retrospect, he saw himself as he had come to Levenford, a gawky youth fresh from college, painfully aware of the deficiencies in his manner, his wardrobe and his medical skill. And though he had no self-pride, he felt a certain satisfaction. In the traditional Scottish manner, he had "improved himself," yet he had changed little. He was the same man, quiet and slow to speak, a little stubborn, perhaps, yet easily touched and given to flaming ardors—hating everything hypocritical.

Ridiculously enough, this story opens with a fishbone. It ends a little less ridiculously with—but you shall see for yourself how it ends.

The fishbone was in the throat of Mr. George McKellor, and one spring evening about nine o'clock Hyslop was called to the McKellor mansion just down the road from Lomond View.

He found McKellor in considerable pain, though not making much fuss, for McKellor was a taciturn, self-contained man. A bachelor by inclination, he had to a marked degree the money sense, and though he was by profession a grain merchant, he was also a successful operator on the stock exchange, and was known to be worth a tidy fortune.

Under the bright light of the handsomely furnished dining room—McKellor had been at his solitary dinner when the mishap occurred—Hyslop made a swift examination. Then, with one deft stroke of his forceps, he removed the offending bone, which was bedded deep down in the soft part of the gullet.

The relief was instantaneous. McKellor swallowed once or twice wryly, then smiled his slow, unwilling smile.

"Must have hurt you a bit," Hyslop remarked, inspecting the jagged bone.

"Ay," replied McKellor, "it was hardly pleasant while it lasted. I must say I'm obliged to ye for looking in so quickly." He paused significantly. "And now—how much do I owe ye, doctor?"

"Oh," said Hyslop, "it was nothing, Mr. McKellor, to run in and tweak it out for you. We'll charge you no fee at all."

McKellar surveyed Hyslop with a queer interest. "Are ye serious?"

"Certainly," returned Hyslop. "It was just a good turn I was able to do you. Perhaps some day you will be able to do one for me."

There was a silence. McKellor stroked his double chin reflectively and finally exclaimed, "Sit down! I'm not minding for any more food. We'll have a drop of Scotch and a crack."

When he had poured the whisky, and they had lighted their pipes, McKellor went on:

"I've heard a good deal about ye, doctor, one way and another, and it hasn't all been to your discredit." A dry smile. "I'm not given to sudden likings, but I tell ye straight I've taken a kind of notion to ye. Forby, as ye say, one good turn deserves another. Tell me, have ye ever heard of Roan Vlei?"

"Never," said Hyslop. "It's a share, I suppose."

"Ay," retorted McKellor. "It's a share, all right—a Kaffir gold mine, to be exact. A few of us have information on the inside, ye ken, about this mine. We've formed a pool. It's in for a big rise. Doctor, I advise ye to buy a few shares of Roan Vlei."

Hyslop laughed. "It's kind of you, Mr. McKellor, but—well, that's not my line of business."

"Ye take my tip," McKellor said, tapping the table in emphasis. "I promise ye'll not regret it."

That same night when Hyslop got home he questioned Cameron about McKellor. "What kind of a man is he? I must say I like him fine."

"Ay, he's one of the best, is McKellor," replied Cameron. "A bit fond o' the siller maybe, but straightforward and honest, and his word is his bond. And since we're speakin' o' siller, he's worth a pickle o't."

Hyslop was impressed by Cameron's dictum. At the start he had not the least idea of following McKellor's advice. He had never set much store on money so long as he had sufficient for his needs, but now there developed in his mind the enticing idea that here was a chance which it would be folly to ignore.

The thought kept hammering away inside his head. He had a nest egg of about five hundred pounds saved up since he had begun his partnership. What was to keep him from doubling—perhaps trebling it?

He slept little that night. All sorts of golden fancies kept flashing before him, and in the morning when he rose he went straight to the telephone.

Catching McKellar before he left for the office, Hyslop told him he intended to purchase five hundred shares of Roan Vlei, which were under a pound a share.

"Right!" said McKellor. Then he added, "Ye're a wise man, doctor. Get in touch with McFarlane, my broker, in Ingram Street. He'll look after ye."

Hyslop had no difficulty establishing contact with McFarlane, and over the telephone the momentous transaction was completed.

The next few days passed in a state of excitement. But nothing happened! There was nothing in the papers; not one word from McKellor. The wretched shares stood at a few pence below the figure at which Hyslop had bought them.

BUT ONE MORNING toward the end of the second week, when he opened the paper, his heart gave a bump. He saw that Roan Vlei had jumped four shillings. Overnight he had made practically one hundred pounds.

He raced to the telephone and rang up McKellor. "I've just seen the news," Hyslop stammered over the wire. "It's great; isn't it? Shall I—shall I sell?"

"What!" McKellar's voice was incredulous. "Sell out at the very beginning? No! Ye wait until I give ye the word."

Flushed and elated, Hyslop went into the surgery and tried to settle to his work. Waiting on him there, very pale and nervous, was Bessie Dallas, who had come for the routine examination demanded by her condition.

Bessie was near her time now, and since it was her first baby, she was pitifully anxious that everything should go all right. Bessie had been the sewing maid at the Marklea Policies—a worthy, capable soul, already in her fortieth year and apparently condemned to spinsterhood—when, to the surprise of everyone, Dallas, one of the gardeners at Marklea, had "up and married" her.

Bessie was happy in her marriage and quietly triumphant that she would shortly confound the prophets by presenting her husband with, she hoped, a son. But because of her age, the case promised to be difficult. For this reason Hyslop had taken special pains to make certain that everything was all right.

This morning the examination, though perhaps a trifle perfunctory, passed off without incident, and Hyslop reassured Bessie. "You're not worrying, Mrs. Dallas?" he chaffed her. "You're as right as rain. In about a week you'll be presenting Dallas with a braw son and heir." And patting her shoulder, he hurried her on her way.

Actually, Hyslop hurried most of his cases during the next few days, so that he might have more time to watch the progress of his speculation. For now Roan Vlei rose like a rocket.

Acting on McKellor's advice, Hyslop increased his holding, buying on margin until he held nearly twelve hundred shares in the Roan Vlei Mine. His profit already stood at over seven hundred pounds, and life was wonderful indeed!

The fact that he had made money so easily mounted like wine to his head. He began to think of all the good things of life which riches could bring him. Why, he would have a cottage at Marklea for the fishing, a new salmon rod, a gig and a fine-stepping cob all to himself.

His work suffered more and more. When not engrossed by the stock market reports, he kept figuring out his profits. Up and up they went. At the end of another four days they stood not far short of nine hundred pounds. Strung to the highest pitch of excitement, he waited for McKellor's final instructions which would make him the possessor of this wealth.

Covertly watching the younger doctor, saying not a word, Cameron gradually assumed an attitude of frowning disapproval. Once or twice he started to speak, but restrained himself. At last, however, at supper on the Thursday of that second week when Hyslop came in late after an interview with McKellor, the old man could stand it no longer.

He darted a glance at Hyslop and growled, "Late again, eh? What's come over ye these days?" He added testily, "Ye can't be still. Ye don't eat, either. And ye look as if ye can't sleep."

"I'll be all right presently," Hy,slop excused himself.

"Presently!" exclaimed Cameron. "And why not immediately?"

"Well," returned Hyslop. "I have something on my mind at the moment."

Cameron rose, rebuke stamped on every lineament. "Ay," he said sternly. "I've a good idea what it is, too, and God knows I don't like it. Let me tell ye plainly ye're not the man I took in partnership. Ye're changin'; ye're losin' your sense of values. And more. Ye're doin' bad work. I'm both disappointed and dissatisfied with it." And Cameron turned and walked out of the room.

Hyslop was cut to the quick by Cameron's rebuke. He felt a pang of compunction. Was he really doing bad work? In a chastened mood he went to bed.

Toward six o'clock on the following morning he was awakened by the long-expected call to Mrs. Dallas's at Marklea. Stung by all that Cameron had said and eager to justify himself, Hyslop answered the summons with alacrity. He tumbled into his clothes, summoned the gig, picked up his bag of instruments and set out on the long drive to Marklea.

The morning was so pure and beautiful that it struck right into Hyslop's heart. Though Jamie, the groom, once or twice attempted a remark, the young doctor was in no mood for conversation. He sat hunched up in his seat, silent.

Neglecting my work, he thought bitterly, between indignation and remorse. Not the man he took in partnership. I'll show him!

In this frame of mind, about two hours later, he reached the Dallas cottage, and here he found an opportunity to test his new-formed resolution.

Mrs. Dallas was already in labor, and it was plain that her time would be severe. Beside her in the little bedroom of the cottage was her mother, Mrs. Thom. Outside, hanging about the back door, was Dallas himself, in a tremble of anxiety.

Without ado Hyslop pulled off his coat, rolled up his sleeves and set to work. There was work in plenty, and there was waiting, too. The forenoon passed quickly and merged into the afternoon. The groans of the patient became deeper and more prolonged. Hyslop stuck manfully to his post, his mind, his whole being, absorbed by the task of saving the mother and the unborn child.

The afternoon drew in; then came at last the moment for drastic action. Taking mask and chloroform, Hyslop put Mrs. Dallas mercifully to sleep. And that was but the beginning. A full hour he labored before the instrumental delivery was complete. And then, alas, it seemed that half his efforts had been in vain. The child came into the world pale and still. A sigh broke from old Mrs. Thom's lips.

"God save us, doctor, the bairn's dead!"

The perspiration was streaming from Hyslop's brow, and there was real worry in his eyes, for the mother herself was in dire extremity.

Snatching the mask from her face, he applied restoratives, and at last succeeded in bringing her round. When she was comfortable, in a passion of haste he turned to the baby.

"Oh, dear, oh, dear!" moaned Mrs. Thom. "To think it should be stillborn, doctor, and a boy, too."

"Bring some hot water," Hyslop shouted, "and cold water as well!" At the same time he began to apply artificial respiration to the apparently lifeless form.

When Mrs. Thom returned with the two full basins he lifted the frail body and plunged it first into the warm water, then into the cold. Again and again he repeated the process, trying to galvanize the child by shock.

He toiled and toiled until, when all seemed lost, a feeble, convulsive gasp tore at the infant's chest.

Hyslop doubled his efforts. Another feeble gasp and another, now less feeble. Then shallow but regular respiration. Triumph swelled in the doctor, and Mrs. Thom gave a cry of thankfulness.

"It breathes, doctor!" she gasped. "Ye've brought the bairn to life!"

Two hours later Bessie Dallas, pale but joyful, with the baby nestling at her breast, whispered to Hyslop, "As a favor, doctor, seein' we owe him to ye, would ye let us call the bairn after ye?"

"If you like," he nodded.

It was nearly five when Hyslop set out on the return drive to Levenford, and almost seven when he reached the outskirts of the town. He felt strangely rested and at peace. But as the gig rattled down High Street, he thought of his Roan Vlei shares and how much they would have risen that day.

He stopped the gig, and dismounting, told Jamie to go home. Proceeding on foot, he bought a paper at the corner of Church Street. Then, as he scanned the financial page, his eyes almost leaped from his head. Across the top of the page stretched a glaring headline: "Bottom Drops Out of Roan Vlei Boomlet."

Hyslop stood a moment facing the incredible position; then with trembling hands he stuck the paper in his pocket and set out for McKellor's house.

He found McKellor waiting for him in the hall, glowing with satisfaction.

"Well, doctor!" he cried. "We did it this time right

enough, eh?"

Hyslop' stared at him, aghast. "Did it? How do you mean?"

"Ye've sold, haven't ye, like I told ye?"

A silence. Then Hyslop muttered, "No, I haven't sold."

"WHAT!" SHOUTED McKellor. "Ye haven't sold? In the name of heaven, why not, man? I rang ye at nine this morning, and left the message. I told ye to sell everything and go a bear on the fall. If ye'd done as I told ye, ye'd have doubled your profit."

There was another heavy silence while Hyslop grasped the situation. "I had a case up at Marklea. I never had your message. I've been away all day."

"Away all day! Didn't I tell ye to keep in touch with me?" McKellor raged. "Wasn't that more important than your miserable case?"

"I don't know," Hyslop said slowly. A pause. Then he added, "I don't think so."

"Ye're a fine man to take trouble over," McKellor said grumpily. "It'll be long before I give ye another tip."

"I don't want it, McKellor," Hyslop answered quietly, and left the house.

He walked home slowly with a somber face, all his ideas of riches shattered.

Cameron was seated by the dining room fire when his young partner came in and flung himself wearily into a chair.

"Ye've had a long day," said Cameron.

"Ay," replied Hyslop, and he told Cameron how the case had gone.

"Well," said Cameron, and his tone was warm with the old friendship, "ye did right to bide there all day." He paused. "But maybe not, though. There's been an uncommon commotion while ye've been away. They were tryin' to get ye from Glasgow all mornin'. Something about buyin' and sellin'." He paused again, significantly. "But I had to tell them ye were busy."

"That's right," Hyslop said slowly. "I was busy." And all at once a great lightness came over him as he remembered the faces of Bessie Dallas and her husband, of the old woman, her mother, and above all, the face of the little child as life stole into it.

During the next few days Hyslop did a lot of hard thinking. When settling day arrived and he received a check showing a balance of a bare ten pounds instead of his original five hundred, he smiled. From the bank he went straight to Jenkins, the jeweler in High Street.

At the end of the interview he said to Jenkins, "It's to be the best solid silver, and it's to cost ten pounds."

A week later a braw christening mug was delivered at the cottage at Marklea, a beautiful mug which made the eyes of Bessie Dallas glisten with delight, a mug which she proudly displayed to the child she held in her arms.

On the mug was inscribed the name:

FINLAY HYSLOP DALLAS

and below were the words:

What money can't buy.

It may be added, finally, that Hyslop's bank balance was never very fat, but Baby Dallas throve enormously.

PROFIT AND LOSS

THE ROAD was up by Overton Terrace, for they were laying new water mains in that select part of the town, and Doctor Finlay Hyslop, returning from a late call on foot, stepped warily to avoid the mud.

"Fine evening, doctor."

Hyslop halted and glanced at the night watchman who was sitting in his little sentry box, surrounded by a banked-up litter of shovels and picks and sledges.

"It *is* a fine evening." The doctor crossed over, emerging from the cold darkness of the October night into the friendly glow cast by the charcoal brazier. Warming his hands, he remarked, "You're cozy, man."

The night watchman laughed. "Dod, and ye're right, doctor. Never was so cozy in my life before."

"You like your new job, then?"

"Like it! Why, I'm fair ta'en with it. I'm thinkin' I've struck it lucky at last."

"Lucky!" Hyslop couldn't help exclaiming. Then he asked, "But don't you find it lonely all night by yourself, being new to it as you are?"

The night watchman shook his head contentedly. "There's all sorts of things to do ye'd never credit, doctor. Things I never bothered about before. It's gey interestin' to have a bit think to yerself under the stars. In the old days I never used to think on anything but the price of a pint or what would win the three-o'clock. But now I think on different things—what makes the dew come down, and for why the flowers aye smell the sweetest at night.

"It fair gets a grip of a man, doctor. And dod! it's excitin', too. Ye ought to see me cookin' my dinner at two o'clock i' the mornin'. Frizzlin' my bacon and boilin' my tea like a gypsy. There never was better bacon nor better tea than what I make on this bit fire here."

"You've turned philosopher, man," the doctor chaffed him. "That's what's wrong with you."

"Maybe ye're right, doctor," the night watchman answered wryly. "But it might have been worse. It wasn't so easy at the beginnin', mind ye, There was a time when I wanted to say to hell with everything, to get drunk, to do any mortal thing to forget. Six months ago, if anybody had told me that I wouldn't regret..."

His voice fell away into silence, as though a memory—a vision—had come upon him. Sitting there under the stars, he gazed in the direction of Langloan

Hill. And Doctor Hyslop, following his eyes, gazed at Langloan Hill, too.

Langloan Hill lies to the west of Levenford, a bare, unbeautiful ridge with a ring of scrubby timber straggling around its base like a fringe of hair on a bald man's skull. But the timber is nothing; the value of the hill lies within. Langloan Quarry, gashing deep into the southern face of the rock, has laid open an escarpment of fine sandstone which has made the hill and its quarry famous.

On one day of the week—usually a Tuesday—as you mount the narrow path which leads from the Ardfillan Road to the hill, you are barred by a little red flag and a notice which says, in red letters: DANGER—BLASTING. Actually, there is little danger in this spot, and if, in defiance of the notice, you choose to push on a few yards you will gain the vantage of the scrubby belt of oaks from where it is possible to observe the blasting operations in detail.

On that particular Tuesday, the twelfth of March, preparations for the forenoon blasting had begun. It was a windy morning; overhead, the clouds scudded across the burnished sky. Two hundred yards away the great red face of the quarry rose sheer. At its base the little squad of drillers were at work.

Dan Tainsh was in charge of the gang. Dan was not the quarry foreman; he was too irresponsible, too unreliable for that. A short, dark, thick-necked fellow with a temper like tinder and a punch like the kick of a mule to back it up, Dan was a bad man to order about. That's why, when on the job, Dan was tacitly admitted to be in charge.

Dan, indeed, might actually have been in charge, but for all his forty-odd years, he seemed never to have learned sense. He drank too much, and his restless, turbulent spirit was always leading him into trouble—yes, even into jail.

"Dan's in the nick again!" The remark became a commonplace among his pals at the quarry when he failed to show up for work at the beginning of the week.

"What for?" someone might ask.

And the reply would come: "Oh, just the usual! Got into a fight with a riveter in the Fitters' Bar. Half killed the poor devil; then turned on the cops. It took three of them to drag him to the jug, drunk an' all as he was."

That was Dan, a ready word and a ready blow—a tormented, surly, bitterly intolerant man who got nothing out of life that seemed to satisfy him.

This morning in particular his mood was black. He used the drill savagely upon the rock and his tongue even more savagely upon his mate, a youngster named Green, who was new to the job.

"Ye'll never make a quarryman," he sneered at the nervous lad. "Spray here, dammit all! Do ye want me to swallow a bucketful of dust?"

Green hurriedly lifted his can and did as he was bid.

"Now, fetch over the soapbox," Dan growled.

"It's back there by the hut."

Young Green gingerly fetched the soapbox, which was Dan's name for the case of dynamite, and stood by while Dan scientifically slipped in the sticks and carefully tamped them home. There were about twenty holes in all—for the blast was to be a big one. Next, Dan adjusted the firing gear, and the whole party went back to the base hut about a hundred yards away.

"Are ye all set, Dan?" inquired Collins, the foreman, who was busy with a time sheet in the hut.

"Ay, we're all set," Dan grunted. "What d'ye think we're here for?"

"Are ye clear at the front end, Joe?" Collins inquired of another man standing with the gang.

Joe Frew, whose duty it was to post the flags and the notices and to inform the gateman at the level crossing, nodded.

Satisfied in his official capacity, Collins picked up his whistle and gave three loud blasts. Then he looked across at Dan. The same moment Dan made contact and fired the shot.

There was a loud, hollow boom, a rapid series of tiny outpuffs from the base of the cliff, then a deep prolonged rumbling. No grand upheaval of rocks into the air that the uninitiated might have looked for. Nothing spectacular. The face of the rock simply slipped away and fell in one cohesive mass, like snow sliding from a house roof in a thaw.

It looked so simple as to be almost silly. Yet hundreds of tons of solid stone crumbled before the eye and fell. A terrific dust rose and still remained when the last reverberating echo had died away.

"A good blast, eh?" Collins exclaimed. He was rather nearsighted, and he peered first at the quarry face and then at Dan.

"It's a bloody bad blast," Dan said disagreeably.

"Look at the near side there." Frew pointed. "It's all undercut."

"Undercut to hell," agreed Dan. And he turned fiercely on Green. "It's all yer fault, ye handless gomeral. That's the end hole I let ye drill. Ye've went in too deep and brung down the whole issue. So help me, I've a mind to wring yer neck."

Green quailed under Dan's glower. "I done my best," he muttered sulkily. "Ye ken I'm only learnin'."

"That's plain as yer ugly mug!"

"Wheesht, man, Dan," Collins propitiated. "We'll gang over and take a look at it."

He came out of the hut, and they all walked over to the cliff face.

"It's not safe, onyway," remarked Frew as they drew near. "We'll need to put a couple of shots above her and bring that owerhung bit down."

The fact was that on the near side, whether through Green's unskillful drilling or through some fault in the sandstone stratum, the shot had undercut. That is, it had brought down the lower masses of the stone without dislodging the upper. Thus a great ledge remained, overhanging the cavity beneath.

Dan, with the others, stopped ten yards away and stood frowning at the botched-up job. From his long experience he knew that it was dangerous; at any instant, down these unsupported tons of rock would crash.

"What a ballox!" He cursed under his breath, and turned to Collins.

At that moment young Green, smarting under what he considered an unjust accusation and burning to justify himself by locating the situation of his borehole, walked straight into the undercut.

A shout from the bunch of men drew Dan around.

"Come out!" Dan roared. "Don't ye know what ye're doin'?"

Green turned and looked at Dan stupidly.

"Come out, ye damned fool!" shouted Dan again. And he dashed in to yank out the flabbergasted lad. That was when the fall occurred. A huge slab of rock broke off the overhanging mass and dropped through the air like an enormous flying tombstone.

Dan heard it, saw it coming. With a powerful effort, he jerked Green out. Then, springing sideways, he tried to get clear. He was a split second too late. The rock, weighing ten tons, fell upon his right leg and mangled it horribly. Dan sprawled on his face. He groaned. He tried to move but could not. His leg, mutilated and useless, was pinned by the stone. He was trapped in the undercut.

A cry of horror and fear went up from the rest of the gang. Collins, Joe Frew and several others dashed into the undercut.

"Get out, dammit!" Dan groaned. "There's more comin' down."

"Wheesht, man, wheesht!" Collins almost blubbered his familiar propitiating phrase as he lifted Dan's shoulders and tried to drag him free.

Dan groaned again. "Ye can't move me. The whole damned graveyard's on top of me."

Joe Frew went down on his knees to lend Collins a hand, but it was hopeless. Dan's leg was fatally imprisoned by the rock.

There was no room to rig tackle that would be strong enough to lift it, and at any minute the entire roof might cave in upon them.

"For God's sake, give us a dram!" Dan said, moistening his lips.

A bottle was hurriedly produced, and at the same time Collins turned to Green.

"Run," he commanded. "Run as quick as you can and bring a doctor, never mind who—get somebody, anybody, Cameron or Hyslop if you can."

The terrified lad took to his heels. At eleven o'clock that forenoon it so happened that Finlay Hyslop went back to Arden House because he had forgotten his stethoscope. But for this unimportant fact he would have been out upon his rounds when Green arrived. As it was, he walked straight into the white-faced, panting youth on the steps. The next minute he was in the gig and was spanking down the road to Langloan.

Over the quarry, when he arrived there, hung that strange, abnormal silence which, in street, shipyard or house, he had come to associate with disaster. Taking his bag of instruments, he sprang out of the gig and hurried toward Dan.

Squeezing himself into the undercut, he made a swift examination. The right leg below the knee was a bloody pulp. There was only one thing to do: amputate.

He looked at Dan, on whose gray face big beads of sweat stood out, and Dan looked back at him. What with the pain and the whisky—for the bottle had been used a lot before the doctor arrived—Dan was a little out of himself.

"Go ahead!" he said. "I know what' ye've got to do—take the bloody thing off. But look slippy, or ye'll get a rock on the back of yer head in the middle o't."

Hyslop made no reply. He flung off his coat, rolled up his sleeves and opened his bag. With a pair of scissors he slit Dan's moleskins, then cut them completely away. He poured half a bottle of iodine over the thigh above the lacerated knee, saturated the mask with chloroform and clapped it over Dan's face.

"I'll get you out of this," he whispered. "Just breathe in and forget about everything."

When Dan was under the influence of the anesthetic, Hyslop propped the bottle against the man's body, tightened the tourniquet and pulled on a pair of rubber gloves. Then he picked up the knife and began.

There was no time for finicking—it was neck or nothing. Lying flat on his stomach under the low roof of the rock, Hyslop worked like a demon, cutting wide flaps, methodically slipping on the artery forceps one after another and slewing round from time to time to drop down to the bone. But as he laid down the saw, a small fragment of stone from the roof fell upon the bottle of chloroform. The bottle smashed, and every drop of the anesthetic flooded upon the ground.

Hyslop gave an exclamation of dismay, but it was impossible to stop now. At frantic speed he went on with the ligatures.

Collins, with his eye on the roof, kept urging him to hurry.

He slipped in two drainage tubes, made good the last internal sutures and started to sew up the flaps with deep stitches. As he threaded his needle for the last time, he suddenly looked around and caught Dan's dilated eye fixed upon him.

"Ye've made a fine job of it, doctor," Dan muttered between his clenched teeth, "though I only saw ye do the hint end of it."

He had been out of the anesthetic for a full five minutes.

As they pulled him clear of the undercut, he tried to speak again, but instead he fainted.

"As I was sayin'," the night watchman went on

meditatively, "six months ago if anybody had told me I wouldn't regret havin' my leg off, I would have bashed him in the jaw—the surly, cantankerous deevil that I was. But somehow, since then, I've taken a different notice about things. I can't tell ye why or how, for I can sit down now and rest without aye wantin' to be on the rampage. I can be quiet. Ay, that's just it. I can be quiet and at peace with myself—a way I never was before. It's queer, but I seem to get more satisfaction out of life with one leg than I did with the twa."

A silence came between the two; then the doctor said, "I suppose it all boils down to this, Dan—that everything happens for the best, though it's hard to realize it at the time. Profit and loss, maybe. What you lose in one way, you gain in another."

Another silence fell. Finally Dan got up, supporting himself on his crutch, and threw some more charcoal on the fire.

"It's a gran', graun' night," said Dan, sniffing the crisp air. "I'd a sight rather be here than in the Fitters' Bar."

They stood for a moment while the still beauty of the night encompassed them. Then Hyslop turned toward the town.

"I'll be off, Dan," he said. "Look out for me tomorrow as I come by." And with echoing footsteps he strode down the road, leaving Dan Tainsh to his silent communion with the stars.

NO IMAGINATION

WILLIE CRAIG rang the bell of Arden House with his usual calmness. "Good evening, Janet," he remarked in his quiet, self-possessed voice. "Does the doctor happen to be at home, by any chance?"

"Which of them were ye wantin' to see, Mr. Craig?"

"It doesna matter in the least, Janet." "It's Doctor Hyslop's night for takin' the surgery. But I'll let Doctor Cameron know ye're here, gin ye wanted specially to see him."

Willie shook his head—slightly, for all Willie's movements were restrained—and said: "It's all one to me, Janet woman."

She gazed at him approvingly. Janet admired a man who never got excited. She showed him into the dining room to wait—a special mark of favor.

Willie sat down and looked with mild interest at the fiddle hanging above the mantelpiece. He was a small, slight man of about thirty-seven, clean-shaven and rather pale, dressed in a neat gray suit and a celluloid collar fitted with a black "made-up" tie.

By trade Willie was a baker; he had his own business in the High Street, where his wife served behind the counter while he worked cheerfully in the bakehouse underneath. Though Willie was well thought of in Levenford, with a name for good baking, fair measure and sound dealing, his reputation was hung upon a higher peg. Willie Craig was famous for his coolness.

"Ay, ay, a cool customer, Willie Craig," was the town's approving verdict.

When, for instance, he played the final of the Winton bowling championship on Levenford Green and won by the margin of a single shot, folks cheered him, not so much because he had won, but because of the manner of his winning. Pale-faced, unruffled, never turning a hair; while Gordon, his opponent, was nearly apoplectic with excitement!

In the Philosophical afterwards, Gordon, with a few drinks inside him, waxed indignant on the subject. "He's not human. He doesn't feel things like other folks do. He's like a fish lying on a block of ice. No imagination! That's the trouble with Willie Craig. He's got no imagination!"

So Willie became known as the man with no imagination; and indeed, he looked stolid enough, sitting there in Arden House waiting to see Finlay Hyslop.

"Will ye step this way, Mr. Craig?" remarked Janet, returning.

He got up and followed her into the surgery.

"Sit down, Willie," said Hyslop. "What's the trouble?"

"It's my tongue, doctor. There's a lump on the edge o't that bothers me a bit."

"You mean, it pains you?"

"Well, more or less."

"Let me have a look." Hyslop took a long look at Willie's tongue. Then he asked, "How long have you had that?"

"Oh, six weeks or thereabouts. It's come on gradual like. But lately it's been gettin' worse."

"Do you smoke?"

"Ay, I'm a pretty heavy smoker."

"A pipe?"

"Ay, a pipe."

There was a pause. Then Hyslop rose and went over to the instrument cabinet. He took a powerful magnifying glass and examined Willie's tongue once again with the most scrupulous care. An angry red spot stood on the edge—a spot which was hard to the touch and, to the young doctor's eye, full of sinister implication.

Hyslop laid down the glass and sank into his chair. There were two ways of dealing with the situation. The first, a specious pretense of optimism; the second, the truth. He gazed at Willie, whose reputation for self-possession he well knew.

Willie gazed back at him calmly. A cool customer, thought Hyslop; not much imagination to trouble him. Yes, I'll let him have the truth.

"Willie," he said, "that little thing on your tongue may be serious."

Willie remained unperturbed. "That's why I'm here, doctor. I want to find out what it is."

"And I want to find out, too," Hyslop replied. "I'll have to take a little snick out of your tongue and send it to the pathological department of the university for microscopic examination. It won't hurt you, and it won't take long. In a couple of days I'll have the result. Then I shall know whether this is what I'm afraid of or not."

"And what are ye afraid of, doctor?"

A bar of silence fell in the consulting room. Hyslop felt he must hedge, but gazing into Willie Craig's cool gray eyes, he changed his mind. In a low voice he said:

"I'm afraid you may have cancer of the tongue."

That bar of silence, scarcely dispelled by those few words, vibrated and again descended, lingering intolerably.

"I see," Willie said. "That's not so good. And what if it should be cancer?"

"Operation," said Hyslop slowly.

"You mean I'd have to have my tongue out?"

"More or less. But we won't face our troubles till we come to them."

For a long time Willie studied the toes of his

boots. Then he raised his head. "Right ye are, then, doctor. Ye'd better get on with what ye got to do."

Hyslop sterilized an instrument, sprayed Willie's tongue with ethyl chloride and skillfully snicked out a tiny fragment.

"That was soon done," Willie said. He washed out his mouth, then picked up his hat, preparing to go.

"Let me see"—Hyslop considered—"it's Monday. Look around on Thursday at the same time, and I'll give you the result."

"I hope it'll be good," Willie remarked.

"I hope so, too," Hyslop answered.

"Good night, then, doctor."

"Good night."

Hyslop watched him go down the drive and into the road, and he muttered: "He's a cool customer, right enough!"

THE COOL CUSTOMER, the man with no imagination, walked along the street, his chin well up, his lips set. Outwardly calm, quite calm! But inside his brain a thousand voices roared and thundered. One word repeatedly endlessly. *Cancer, cancer, cancer.*

He felt his heart thudding tumultuously against his side. As he turned into Church Street a spasm of giddiness assailed him.

"How do, Willie? Fine evening for the Green!" Bailie Paxton hailed him from across the street.

Not one man, surely, but a row of them, all waving, grimacing, shouting, "Cancer, cancer, cancer!"

"A fine evening it is, Bailie."

"We'll see ye on Saturday at the match."

"Ye will, indeed. I wouldna miss it for a ransom." How in the name of God had he managed to speak?

As he moved off, a cold sweat broke upon him. The muscles of his cheek began to twitch. His whole being dissolved, defying at last his constant vigilance.

All his life long he had fought like a demon against his nerves—those treacherous nerves which had so often threatened to betray him. He had found it difficult, always, even the little things. That time, for instance, when he had won the bowling championship, so sick inside with apprehension he could scarcely throw his final wood, yet managing to mask his nervous terror with indifference.

But now, faced with this awful thing . . . Oh, how could he face it?

He entered his house quietly—his house above the shop, which was now shut; he sat down, pulled on his slippers.

"Ye're early back from the Green, Will," Bessie, his wife, remarked pleasantly, without looking up from the local paper.

At all events, with Bessie, he simply mustn't show anything. "I didn't bother about the Green tonight. I just took a bit dauner down the road."

"Uh-huh! These are awful nice hats Jenny M'Kechnie's advertising. I've a guid mind to treat myself to one."

Staring into the fire, Willie made an unbelievable

effort to master himself. "It's time ye were buyin' something for yerself."

She flashed a warm smile at him. "Maybe I will, then, and maybe I'll not. I never was one to squander money on finery. No, no. I'm not wanting us to be stuck here over the shop all our lives. A semidetached villa up Barloan way—what do ye say to that in a year or two?"

In a year or two! The simple words transfixed him, like a sword thrust savagely into his breast. A year or two! Where would he be then? He closed his eyes, fighting back smarting tears.

Bessie laughed. "A lot of difference it makes to ye, ye auld sinner! There's nothing on earth would put ye up or down."

He went to bed early, but he could not sleep. He was still awake when Bessie came to bed, although, in order that he might not have to speak, he pretended to be asleep.

Lying there with tightly shut eyes, he listened in agony to her familiar movements: winding the clock; dropping hairpins into a tray. Then quietly, for fear of disturbing him, she slipped into bed.

He lay quite still, scarcely breathing, clenching his hands fiercely to control himself. He wanted to cry out, to ease his tortured nerves by one despairing shout.

He wanted to turn to Bessie, to implore her sympathy, to cry passionately, "I'm not what you think I am! I'm not hard. I never have been hard. I feel everything terribly. And now I'm frightened, desperately frightened. I've always been sensitive, always been nervous. That's why I've pretended not to be. But now I'm past pretending. Don't you understand? They think—they think I've got cancer!"

At that dreadful word, though it remained unspoken, a paroxysm of agony shook him. He thrust his hands upon his mouth to choke back the sobs.

The dark hours of night rolled over him. Not for one moment did he sleep. Not for one second did he forget.

At four o'clock he rose, put on his working clothes and went into the bakehouse. He hoped the routine of the day might soothe him, distract his mind. But it was not so. As the day passed, he grew more desperate. Outwardly frozen, he went through his duties in the semblance of normality.

He *knew* now that he had cancer.

That night again he did not sleep. At breakfast his wife turned upon him a mildly solicitous eye.

"Ye're off yer food these past few days."

"Nonsense!" he protested; and to prove his words, he helped himself to more bacon and an egg.

All his senses were numb now except the sense of his own condition. He was, perhaps, a little mad. His imagination, working feverishly, carried him a stage further. The fact that he had cancer was accepted, proved. What was to be done, then? Operation, the doctor had said.

He saw himself in the hospital in a narrow bed. He

watched himself being wheeled to the operating theater. What was the stuff they gave you there? Chloroform—that was it. A sickly, pungent stuff that hurried you into oblivion.

But what happened in that oblivion? Sharp lancets flashed about his mouth. They were cutting out his tongue. A sob rose in his throat, choking him.

And after the operation? He would awake in that same narrow bed, an object of sympathy and intolerable solicitude. A man who could not speak.

OH, IT WAS terrible, terrible—not to be endured! He lost himself in the agony of the thought.

Wednesday night passed—it might have been a hundred years! Thursday came. He had come almost to the limit of his suffering—such suffering as no one dreamed of, all concealed within his soul.

After lunch on Thursday he walked down to the river. It was high tide, and the water, rushing past the quayside, lay but a few feet beneath him. He stared at it stupidly. One step and it would be finished—all his wretchedness. The river, gurgling against the stone piers, seemed to call him.

Suddenly he heard a voice at his elbow. "Taking a breath of air, Willie man?"

It was Peter Lennie smiling at him.

As in a dream he heard himself reply, "It's pretty hot in the bakehouse in the afternoon."

They stood in silence. Then Peter Lennie said, "I'll walk down the road with ye if ye're going that way."

They talked as they strolled along the quayside. There was no escape for Willie. He had to go on.

The afternoon passed. He drank a cup of tea; then, going upstairs, changed into his Sunday clothes. His mind was made up now. He would refuse to have the operation. He had resolved to die.

At half past six he told Bessie he would take a little stroll. As he walked down Church Street he had the strange sense of unreality of a man walking with ghostly steps to his own funeral.

"Is the doctor in, Janet?"

He was saying it again, that silly, senseless phrase. Yes! He was sitting in the dining room again, staring at the fiddle that hung above the mantelpiece.

And then once again he was in the consulting room, standing before the desk as though he stood before the judgment seat of God.

Hyslop looked at him a long, long time. Then, rising, he held out his hand. "I want to congratulate you, Willie Craig. I've had the full pathological report. There isn't a trace of malignancy. It's a simple irritation of your tongue. With treatment, it will be gone in a couple of weeks."

Willie's senses reeled. A great wave of joy broke over him. He could have swooned from the ecstasy of joy and relief; but his calm face showed nothing.

"I'm obliged to ye, doctor," he said. "I'm—I'm—I'm real glad it's no waur."

"I hope you haven't been worried," Hyslop persisted. "Of course, I'd never have let you know what I was afraid of if I hadn't been certain you weren't the worrying kind."

"Thut's all right, doctor," Willie murmured. "Maybe I'm not the worryin' kind." That quiet, self-contained smile of his played over his face as he added, "They aye say that's my trouble, ye ken. No imagination!"

CONDUCT UNBECOMING

NO MAN is a hero to his biographer. And if the biographer be honest, he will display the defects of his character parallel with his merits, balance his vanities fairly against his virtues.

Do not imagine, then, that Finlay Hyslop was the Admirable Crichton of Levenford society, a blameless young medico who was never stupid, fatuous or foolish. Once in a while Hyslop was all three. And that is why you must hear about Miss Malcolm.

He met Miss Malcolm at a dance during his first months in Levenford. Not, mark you, an ordinary dance, like the Burgh Hall hop, but the annual private dance given by the Sinclairs.

The Sinclairs, of course, were the shipbuilding people whose yards outrivaled even the famous shipyards of the Rattrays. They were county people, whose estate between Levenford and Ardfillan was the pride and envy of the countryside.

Every winter they gave a dance—a ball, to be accurate—at which everybody who was anybody appeared. To this affair, by way of indicating the liberalism of the gentry, were invited the best professional people of the district—the "best-thought-of" doctors, lawyers, and their wives.

It came about, then, that a large gilt-edged card arrived at Arden House bidding Doctors Cameron and Hyslop to the ball.

"Bah!" said Cameron as he tossed it on the mantelpiece. "I'll miss my night's sleep for none of them. Ye can go, man. My dancing days are done."

Hyslop protested that he had as much use for a ball as a bull for a china shop.

"Ye'd better look in, though, lad," Cameron answered in a more equable tone, "if only for the matter of policy. The Sinclairs can put many a guinea yer way if they choose to think on't. Just ye drop in about ten; let yerself be seen hobnobbing with his Grace"—Cameron's eyes twinkled—"sup an ice with her Leddyship, tell the member I thought his last speech was trash, and then come home to yer bed."

So Hyslop did go to the dance.

At first he did not enjoy himself; he was, in fact, unhappy and extremely ill at ease. On the stairs there was a great press of people with Roman noses and high voices, a delirious clash of clan tartans with scarlet jackets on the floor, and a strong sense of superiority in the air. No one took the slightest notice of him.

Though he doggedly called up all his democratic pride to support him, he gradually became aware of himself as an unfledged provincial doctor who knew nobody, and whom nobody wished to know. But he set himself dourly to stick it out, feeling horribly lonely, trying hard to despise the petty affectations displayed before him, but despising only himself.

It was then he discovered two friendly brown eyes fixed upon him. His color deepened; but the lady smiled at him, and he smiled back. He felt sure he had seen her before. Then he remembered. With a certain confidence he went over to where she sat underneath a tall green palm. She received him with perfect ease.

"You're Doctor Hyslop," she informed him charmingly. "I know you quite well, though we've never been introduced. But you haven't the least idea who I am."

"But I have! You're Miss Malcolm." He almost added "the schoolteacher," but mercifully restrained himself in time.

She had been a schoolteacher, for all that; had taught French at St. Hilda's, the most exclusive girls' school in Ardfillan. But she had come into a little money of her own, and while quite young had given up her profession.

She smiled at him again and made room for him to sit beside her. At that he felt comfortable.

"I'm surprised to find you here," he remarked confidentially, thinking unconsciously once again of her social status which was—well, inferior even to his own.

"I'm often surprised to find myself here," she admitted. She had a delightful voice—well modulated and soft. "It's a nuisance, but in a sense I find myself bound to come. You see, Matthew Sinclair is my cousin."

His face was a study. A cousin of Sir Matthew Sinclair! She was one of them, related by blood to the head of the clan, and he had attempted to patronize her!

"You're not dancing?" She appeared not to have observed his confusion, but kept beating time to the music with her tiny ivory fan.

"I'm such a wretched dancer," he said.

She smiled. "Shall we try?"

They tried. She was a magnificent dancer, light in his arms as a thistledown. After the first moment of hesitation he enjoyed the dance marvelously.

"That was glorious," he said boyishly as they resumed their seats.

"We might have another," she suggested. "But first you might fetch me an ice. Chocolate, please."

He dashed to the buffet and brought her back a chocolate ice.

She ate it in silence, nodding to people as they swung past. He watched her admiringly.

She was a lady. Yes, she was a lady.

And she was—how could he phrase it?—she was *quite* good-looking. Her brown eyes sparkled; the dance had brought a faint flush to her cheeks; she wore a charming white flounced frock—simple and girlish. And she was not very old.

How old was she, exactly? Puzzled, he tried to guess. Thirty, perhaps; certainly not a day more than thirty-five.

He said suddenly, in a low voice, "It's more than decent of you to bother with an idiot like me. Do you realize that before we met I hadn't spoken to a single soul here but the butler? And he just drooped his eyelids at me like a bishop."

She went into a peal of laughter, then said solemnly, "That's because you don't know anybody. We must change all that."

In five minutes she introduced him to half a dozen men. They were not snobs, but decent fellows, after all, he saw. He was no longer an outsider.

The women to whom she made him known were—quite by chance, of course!—too old to dance. But that didn't matter in the least. It was her he wished to dance with. Their steps matched perfectly. Hyslop had a grand evening. He returned to Levenford, not at eleven, as Cameron had predicted, but at four o'clock on the following morning. Before he left Sinclair House he asked Miss Malcolm if he might see her home. She shook her head prettily.

"I'm staying here overnight, but you must come to see me when I get back to my house. You know where it is. In that funny old crescent behind Levenford Park. Come in the evening when you have time. In the evening I'm usually free."

Next morning at breakfast Hyslop was fresh as a daisy, and full of the dance.

Old Cameron looked at him. "It takes youth," he observed, "to dance all night and get up next mornin' without swearin' at the porridge. Ye seem to have had a gran' time."

"A glorious time," the young doctor agreed.

"Did ye meet many of the folks?"

"Met tons of people."

"Do ye tell me now! That's gran'. Maybe Sir Matthew'll be havin' ye in next time he takes the measles."

Hyslop colored. "As a matter of fact," he observed loftily, "I danced most of the evening with Sir Matthew's cousin!"

"Sir Matthew's cousin?"

"Exactly! With Miss Malcolm."

"Miss Malcolm!" Cameron echoed blankly, then covered his amazement by falling hastily on his kipper. "Ay, ay, she is some connection of the Sinclairs. Not a first cousin, I shouldn't say; no, hardly as near as that. But a nice-enough body."

"She is, indeed. A charming girl! I must look her up one day soon."

Cameron scraped back his chair decisively. "Ye're far too busy for any such damned thing. Ye're a working doctor, man, not a blasted troubadour."

It was curious, in the light of that remark, that Hyslop was run off his legs for the next few days. For an entire fortnight not one moment of leisure did he have in which he might have called to see Miss Malcolm. At the end of that period, however, a note arrived, smelling delicately of verbena:

"I had expected you to come to see me as a friend. Now, alas, I must invoke you as a doctor! I am not quite well. Nothing serious. But a nuisance, rather. Come in the evening if you can, and I shall give you coffee."

Hyslop sniffed the note. What a charming perfume! So she was ill, poor soul, and he had neglected her shamefully. Ah, it was too bad.

"There's a call for Miss Malcolm," he informed Cameron at lunchtime.

Cameron's brows jerked up. But he said nothing.

"I'll do it, of course," Hyslop went on. A pause. "I'll go round to see her—"

"In the evening!" shouted Cameron, and began to sip his broth like a lunatic.

Hyslop admired Miss Malcolm's house the moment he entered it. It was a gracious old home of weathered red sandstone. The rooms were large and spacious, and the furnishing was in keeping with the whole.

Miss Malcolm had traveled widely and had picked up many pieces. "You like my painted chest? It is rather good. I got it from a funny little *Gasthof* in the Tirol." Or: "These old candlesticks. They're Quimper ware. I bought them from the dearest old Breton woman in Val-André."

Miss Malcolm was in the drawing room reclining in a long chair beside the fire. An old silver tray with Spode china and a Georgian coffeepot stood at her elbow.

"Faithless one!" she exclaimed brightly. "If I hadn't been ill, I should never have seen you again."

"I've been wanting to come round," he protested, "but I've been so busy. Tell me, though, what's the trouble?"

"I think I danced too much the other night. My heart—it's nothing, of course—a mere nothing."

Full of concern, he examined her heart. There was not much wrong that he could make out—a faint murmur, perhaps, but no perceptible lesion. He straightened, addressed her solicitously.

"You must rest. That's it. You must rest for a bit. And I'll make you up a tonic. Trust me. I'll look after you."

She thanked him, adding, "Ever since I went climbing in Arosa I've been bothered. I'm perfectly strong, of course. Perfectly sound."

While she gave him coffee he talked to her of climbing in Switzerland, which they agreed he would adore. The coffee was delicious. She begged him to smoke his pipe. She adored a pipe.

Then they talked of travel; of the fascinating, exotic places of the East; of books. She talked intelligently, wittily. He gazed at her admiringly. Under the softly shaded lights she looked quite beautiful.

She was on the thin side, it is true, and her liquid brown eyes were big, full, even prominent. The skin of her neck had a dry look, and her nose, from certain angles, had a queer sharpness. But she had a way of animating her features which dispelled critical analysis.

Hyslop thought her a most delightful, stimulating person. She gave him a sense of his own value.

It was ten o'clock when, reluctantly, he rose to go.

The following evening came, and he "looked in" to see Miss Malcolm. The next evening, too, and the next. They were professional visits, she emphatically insisted, and every time, before coffee and conversation, Hyslop listened to her heart.

About ten days later Cameron came to Hyslop in the dispensary. He hummed and hawed, then abruptly declared: "Ye're callin' pretty often to see Miss Malcolm!"

"Why, yes," said Hyslop, surprised. "She's knocked up her heart a little."

"Her heart?" Cameron echoed drily. "So they're all professional visits."

"Certainly!" Hyslop exclaimed indignantly. "What are you looking at me like that for? I've done nothing unprofessional. But if you want the truth, I enjoy going to see Miss Malcolm immensely."

"Are ye in love with the damned woman?" Cameron demanded violently.

Hyslop flushed. "She's not a damned woman! She's a lady! And I'm extremely attracted to her."

Cameron threw up his hands. "My God!" he groaned. "And I thought ye had sense."

That evening Hyslop went around determinedly to Miss Malcolm's house. Cameron's attitude made him all the more stubborn. He gave her hand an extra pressure; said how glad he was to see her. Then he took out his stethoscope.

There might have been a different ending to this tale if Miss Malcolm had only kept her head, but carried away by Hyslop's extra cordiality, she flung her arms round his neck.

"I can't help it, Finlay," she murmured. "You're too sweet for words!" And she kissed him on the lips.

Hyslop recoiled. "Y-you mustn't," he stammered. "You mustn't do that."

Everything in his training revolted at the idea. A patient's arms round his neck. Conduct unbecoming in a professional respect. A man might be struck off the register for less.

Panic seized him. He blurted out an excuse and bolted from the room. He went straight to Cameron and told him everything.

Cameron looked at him. "So ye've had yer lesson at last, my lad! Now that ye're in a condition to understand, how old do ye think yer braw Miss Malcolm is?"

"I don't know," Hyslop mumbled.

"She's forty-two if she's a day. Forty-two! And she's been lookin' for a man these past four-and-twenty years. Listen! Have ye ever seen her in the mornin'?"

"No," said Hyslop feebly. "She's always asked me to come—"

"In the evening," Cameron cut in. He paused impressively. "But if you'd seen her in the mornin' . . ." And that was all.

Next day Cameron paid the visit to Miss Malcolm. He went in the morning, and he didn't stay long.

But the odd fact is that Miss Malcolm's strained heart got better immediately.

JUDGMENT OF THE GODS

IT MAY HAVE been providence, or it may have been mere chance, but there was a strange fatality about the affair at Shawhead that made a deep impression on Finlay Hyslop. He never forgot it.

In the spring of the year an epidemic of scarlet fever occurred round the Barloan Toll which caused him serious anxiety. It started in the month of May, a severe form of the disease, affecting chiefly the younger children of the district, and it showed no signs of abating.

As the weeks passed, and one case rapidly followed another despite all his efforts, Hyslop set himself to discover the origin of the epidemic. He expected no help from the public health authorities. At this time the post of medical officer of health to Levenford was vested in the small but self-important person of Doctor Snoddie, who regarded his office as a sinecure and was content to draw his honorarium of fifty guineas a year without exerting himself to earn it.

For about a week Hyslop made careful observations, and he came to a positive conclusion.

There was one point common to all the cases he had met, and that was the milk supply, which came in every instance from the farm adjacent to Barloan, known as Shawhead. The more he analyzed it, the more Hyslop was convinced that the Shawhead milk was spreading the disease. He had no proof, of course, merely his instinct, but it was enough to make him resolve to act at once.

On the forenoon of the following Tuesday he called at Shawhead. It was a pretty place, with whitewashed farm buildings against which rambler roses were already beginning to bloom. Everything, as far as the eye could see, was sweet and clean.

Small wonder it was that Rab Hendry should be proud to own this farm, with its fine dairy and the herd of pedigreed Jersey cows which often won him prizes.

Known colloquially as "Shawhead"—taking the name from the land that was his patrimony—Rab was something of a character: a big, dark, craggy man of about fifty, with iron-gray hair, a bellowing voice and a fist like a ham. Shawhead's whole life was bound up in his farm and his young wife Jeannie, whom he had recently married.

When Hyslop knocked at the green door of the farmhouse it was Jeannie who answered it; but at his question she smiled and shook her head.

"No," she answered "the good man's out. He's gone to Ardfillan market with some beasts. He'll not be back till this afternoon."

She was a bonny thing, the new mistress of Shawhead, plump and brisk, with pink cheeks and lovely coppery hair braided trimly behind her ears. She was as neat and clean as a new pin, and as Hyslop surveyed her against the background of the well-kept farm, his suspicions began to waver.

"So Shawhead's out," he temporized.

"Ay," she answered. "But he'll be home the back of four. Will ye look in then, or is there any message I could give him?"

"I'll look in," Hyslop said. And then he added awkwardly, "As a matter of fact, Mrs. Hendry, it's not exactly pleasant business I've come about. I'm worried over the epidemic of scarlet fever roundabout, and I find that in all my cases—well, not to put too fine a point on it, every time the milk has come from Shawhead." He paused. "I wondered if I might look into things to see if by any chance the cause of the trouble might be here."

At his words her face clouded. "The fever!" she cried indignantly. "To mention it even in the same breath with our good milk! I never heard such impudence! To be sure, Doctor Hyslop, if it's that ye've come about, ye'd better see the master."

And she shut the door in Hyslop's face.

Discouraged by this setback and annoyed, Hyslop continued his round.

He had half a mind to let the matter drop, but at the very next house he found that the Lennox boy, one of his fever cases, had taken a turn for the worse, and that the lad's brother showed signs of sickening.

Hyslop determined not to abandon his original purpose. In fact, at midday, when he got home, he mentioned his intention to Cameron.

"It looks like the milk, right enough," the older doctor said slowly, "when ye reason it out that way. And yet I can't think it, either. Shawhead has a model place." He paused. "Go and see him, but be careful how ye set about it. He's a touchy deevil; his temper's like tinder."

That afternoon Hyslop returned to Shawhead Farm and knocked once again on the green door. There was no answer, and imagining that Shawhead might be at work, Hyslop wandered across the yard and into the byre.

As he entered, the byreman was bringing in the cows in preparation for the evening milking. Hyslop observed the fine, sleek animals as they took their places in the stalls. He then watched the byreman, Douglas Orr, known familiarly as "Dougal," take the three-legged stool, and begin the milking.

Hyslop's eyes dwelt in fascination upon Dougal, for the youth had a pale, sickly look, and around his throat a twist of red flannel. Hyslop greeted him, and Dougal looked up.

"I'd no idea you were here, doctor. Are you after a glass of milk?"

Hyslop shook his head. "I'll have no milk today, Dougal." And then, "What's the matter with your neck?" He indicated the red flannel.

Dougal gave a conscious laugh. "Oh, it's nothing. I had a sore throat some weeks past, and it's left me kind of poorly."

Hyslop's gaze became more intent. "A sore throat!" he echoed; then, "Did you have any rash with the sore throat?"

"Rash!" echoed Dougal. "And what might that be?"

Hyslop started to explain; then he caught sight of Dougal's hands. There was no need to seek further.

His eyes were grave as they dwelt on Dougal's hands, for from each of them the particles of skin were peeling.

HYSLOP RECOGNIZED the evidence instantly. It was unmistakable—the fine branny desquamation which invariably follows scarlet fever, which, coupled with the sore throat, convinced the doctor that Dougal had had the disease, in a mild form, perhaps, but sufficiently active to be the focus of the epidemic which had ravaged the district.

Suddenly a loud voice broke the stillness and caused Hyslop to look up. "So ye're here, are ye? Spying and shoving yer nose into other people's business!"

It was Shawhead, dark with anger, fists clenched. Behind him stood Jeannie.

It was a painful moment, but Hyslop confronted the man. "I'm sorry, Shawhead. I'm not here from choice. It's plain necessity." He pointed to the byreman. "Douglas has had scarlet fever, probably a mild attack, but enough to do a lot of damage. It looks as if you might have to shut up your dairy for a week or two."

"What!" roared Shawhead. "Ye dare say that to me?"

"Be reasonable, Shawhead," Hyslop pleaded. "I know you have a tidy place, but the fact remains that it's here the infection has come from."

"The infection!" choked Shawhead. "From here! How dare ye say that? We're all clean folks at this farm."

"Yes, but Dougal—" protested Hyslop.

"Dougal's as clean as the rest of us!" cried Shawhead. "He's had a bit sore throat and no more. It's insanity to make out we must shut up because o't."

"I tell you that he's had scarlet fever," persisted Hyslop. "He's scaling. That's what is contaminating your milk."

The veins of Shawhead's forehead almost burst with passion. "That's enough!" he shouted. "The very idea! My fine milk contaminated! It's bonny sweet milk, and always has been. There's people glad to drink it. I'll show ye!"

And in an access of fury he seized the dipper and plunged it into the milk. Raising the brimming measure in a gesture of defiance, he drank half of it himself, then gave the dipper to Jeannie. She smiled and quaffed the milk to the last drop.

"There!" went on Shawhead. "That'll show ye what we think of our milk. My wife drinks it, and I drink it. And ye dare to say another word against it, I tell ye plain ye'll bitterly regret it."

"I'm sorry you've taken it this way," said Hyslop. "You make it hard for me. But I've got to fight you."

Hyslop went straight to Doctor Snoddie, put the whole case before the little man and demanded that he take steps immediately to meet the situation.

Snoddie peered at Hyslop, delighted that the younger man should have come more or less to beg a favor of him. He had little love for Hyslop since his humiliation over the case of Alexander Deans, and his petty nature rose exultantly to grasp this opportunity to get back at the young doctor.

"I'll look into it, of course," he remarked in a patronizing tone. "But frankly, I cannot see that you have any grounds for your accusation. There's no positive evidence—no rash, no fever. You must remember that it's a serious matter asking any man to close his dairy on what may be merely an unfounded conjecture."

Hyslop flushed hotly. "Conjecture be hanged!" he cried. "That byreman is the focus of infection. I'm not asking you to do it as a favor. I'm telling you it's your duty to close the Shawhead dairy!"

"Indeed!" said Snoddie. "Well, I'll look into it

when I have time. You'll hear from me in a day or so."

Though Hyslop fretted under this petty manifestation of officialdom, he had to make the best of it and wait for Snoddie's decision. He said nothing to Cameron, but on the following day, as they sat at lunch, the note arrived.

Hyslop read it, and let out a cry of indignation. He tossed the paper over to Cameron. "Have a look at that! Of all the incompetent weaklings!"

The note was from Snoddie, and it stated curtly that after full investigation of the facts the medical officer of health of Levenford saw no grounds whatever for closing the Shawhead Dairy Farm.

"Ye're sure of yer facts about Dougal?" Cameron questioned.

"As sure as I'm sitting in this room."

"Well," sighed Cameron, "It's what ye might expect of Snoddie. But we can do nothing about it. We must sit tight and hope for the best."

"And let this contaminated milk set up a dozen more cases? No, thanks!" cried Hyslop, jumping up. "I'll be hanged if I do! If we can't lick them officially, we'll do it the other way. I'll tell every patient I have in Barloan that I suspect Shawhead's milk. I'll get the news around."

Roused to stubborn pugnacity, the young doctor was as good as his word.

In the course of his visits he mentioned, guardedly but emphatically, his doubts about the Shawhead milk supply. In no time at all word went around Barloan, which was the district chiefly supplied by Shawhead, and in a couple of days the place rang with Hyslop's word. People took sides, tongues wagged, and the thing became the chief matter of interest in the town.

Conscious that he was doing no more than his duty, Hyslop stuck grimly to his guns, but on Friday of the same week a document arrived which shook him. It was a writ for slander, issued by Shawhead through Logan, a local solicitor.

Hyslop took the ominous parchment to Cameron, who studied it in silence.

"I was feared something like this might happen," said Cameron. "He's a bitter man, Shawhead, when he's roused."

"I can justify myself!" cried Hyslop. "You know I acted for the best."

"Well," said Cameron, "that's what ye must tell the court."

SLIGHT ENCOURAGEMENT, perhaps, for Cameron said no more, yet Hyslop knew the older man was behind him. Nevertheless, as the days went on and he realized that he must go into court to face the charges made against him by Shawhead, a tremor of apprehension went through him.

Another day passed, and another. On the third afternoon, as Hyslop sat moodily in the surgery, Cameron came in with consternation written on his face.

"Have ye heard the news?" he cried. "She's down

with acute scarlet fever. Shawhead's wife, Jeannie."

One astounded instant. Then, in a flash, Hyslop remembered Shawhead's defiant gesture as he passed Jeannie the dipper of milk, which she drank. There could be no doubt now. Surely it was positive proof of his contention!

"Don't ye see?" said Cameron. "This justifies ye to the hilt. They'll never go on with the case now. Why, man, they tell me Shawhead's near off his head with grief and anxiety. It's a judgment."

Hyslop said, "Yes, it's a judgment, maybe. Maybe it's come from a higher court."

Levenford gasped at the sensational turn of events, and opinion swung in favor of the young doctor. He became at one stroke protector of the people and the public health of Levenford. But he would have none of the congratulations which folks tried to offer him, for news had come that Jeannie Hendry was desperately ill.

Shawhead had forbidden her removal to the hospital, and now in truth was the dairy closed, the whole farm isolated.

Snoddie, worried, was in close attendance, and a specialist had been summoned from Glasgow. In spite of all this, Jeannie Hendry grew worse. On Sunday it was reported that she was sinking.

On the evening of that Sabbath, Janet the housekeeper entered the sitting room where Cameron and Hyslop both sat. Her voice was low as she said, "It's all done with now. Jamie just brought the news.

Shawhead's wife—she's dead."

Six weeks later, Hyslop met Shawhead for the first time since his bereavement. The farmer, utterly broken by his loss, was returning from the cemetery.

Hyslop stopped, and almost mechanically Shawhead stopped, too. The eyes of the two men met, and each read in the face of the other the knowledge of what might have been—the terrible knowledge that if Shawhead had submitted to Hyslop's advice, his wife might now have been alive beside him.

A groan burst from the pale lips of the farmer, and he thrust out his hand, which met Hyslop's in an anguished grasp of friendship and remorse.

THE MAN WHO CAME BACK

ONE EVENING in early June as Finlay Hyslop sat in his surgery, there entered a man whom he had never seen before in Levenford. The stranger was perhaps between thirty-five and forty years old, but it was uncertain, for his features, lean, haggard and jaundiced by tropic suns, wore that look of cheap experience which puts the stamp of age upon the face of youth.

The manner of this young-old man was easy, flashy, almost arrogant. He was dressed in a light suit of ultra-sporting cut, carried worn-out yellow gloves and a chipped Malacca cane, while his hat lay on the back of his head as if to mask the stains upon its threadbare nap by this extremely rakish tilt.

"Evening, doctor sahib," remarked the unusual visitor with complete assurance; and without invitation he flung himself into the chair beside Hyslop's desk. "Dropped in on you to get acquainted. I'm

Hay—Bob Hay, Esquire, of the North East India Company. Just back from Bombay to look the old town up again."

Hyslop stared at the queer individual in surprise. He started to put a question, but before he could speak Hay resumed.

"Pretty damn funny the old town looks after fifteen years. I can tell you, when a man's been out East and seen the world, he's fit to laugh his sides out at a *chota* spot like this. Ha! Ha! Call it the royal and ancient burgh. It's ancient, all right. No life, doc; no bright lights; nothing! Damn my liver! I don't know how I'll stand it, now I've come home."

With growing repugnance, Hyslop studied the flashy Hay—Bob Hay, Esquire, as he styled himself—this son of Levenford, returned to his native town after many years abroad. At last he inquired brusquely, "Seeing that you find it so unsatisfactory, may I ask you why you came back?"

Bob Hay laughed.

"Reasons of health, doctor sahib! Climate plays the devil with a man's liver and lights out East. And the life, y'know: dinners, dances, regimental balls. When a man's run after socially—oh, you understand how it is, old man! Had to give it up for a bit and come back. Couple of my pals in Bombay, big specialists out there, advised me to have a little rest and perhaps take a trip home."

A pause, while Hyslop grappled with this information. "You're returning to India, then?" he queried.

"Maybe, maybe," evaded Hay. "We'll see how we get on in the old home town. Might settle down here; buy a little estate up the country. Y'never know. Company have been handsome, hang it all! Settled a whacking pension on Bobbie Hay!"

"They've pensioned you?" echoed Hyslop.

For all his airy pretense, if Hay had been pensioned by his company, it was plain he would never go back to India. But why? Hyslop stared with a new intentness at the other man, whose pinchbeck outer husk revealed, on closer examination, the manifest seediness beneath. And scrutinizing closely, Hyslop became aware of a sickly pallor underlying the sunburnt complexion, of a shortened breathing, a restless tremor of the thin fingers.

Decisively he pulled a sheet of paper toward him and picked up his pen. "We seem to be wasting time. Do you wish to consult me, or what exactly can I do for you?"

"Oh, nothing much, doctor sahib," protested Hay with a deprecating gesture. "I don't want to consult you. And don't bother about particulars or medicine. I've a prescription from my Bombay pals I take when I remember. As a matter of fact, I only looked in because the company asked me to see my doctor sahib at home. I shall have to send them a medical chit from you every month." He paused. "Because of my pension, don't you see?"

"No," returned Hyslop, "I don't see. I cannot undertake to give you a certificate unless I know what's the matter with you. If you want a certificate from me, you'll have to let me examine you."

There was a curious pause; then out came Hay's ready laugh. "Right you are, then, old sport. I don't mind."

He rose and slipped off his coat and vest, revealing the shabbiest of underclothing. Stripped, his ribs stood out like spars, while in the center of his narrow chest there moved a curious pulsation.

Hay's whole bodily appearance indicated a wasted, ill-spent life. But Hyslop's eyes remained riveted upon that pulsing, ominous movement in the breast.

Hyslop made a careful examination, sat down at his desk again and remarked: "You can dress now; that's all, for the moment. I'll give you a certificate."

"Right you are, doctor sahib!" cheerfully exclaimed Hay. "Knew that there wouldn't be the slightest difficulty. Old warhorse is fit as a fiddle. I'll be all right, once I dig up a little sport and gaiety in this one-anna town."

Hyslop did not answer; he continued writing the certificate. But when Hay was dressed, he said: "Sport and gaiety are not for you, Hay. You're a sick man. You must have complete rest and freedom from all excitement."

"Ah, a lot of tommyrot, doc," laughed Hay. "I'm right as rain."

"You're not right," Hyslop repeated with emphasis. "Don't you realize you're suffering from advanced aneurysm of the aorta?"

As the fatal name of that awful complaint echoed in the surgery, again that curious silence fell. Then Hay smiled, though this time the smile was somewhat ragged. He stared at Hyslop defiantly, revealingly. But only for an instant. The ready laugh rang out again.

"That's a good one, doctor sahib. But you can't scare me with those fancy tales. Ha! Ha! The lad's hard as nails and tough as leather. The old pump's out of gear a bit, that's all. Nothing serious." And picking up the certificate, he tucked it into his pocket, nodded to Hyslop confidently and strolled out.

Hyslop sat at his desk frowning, surprised at Hay's indifference to the dreadful malady which possessed him.

Could the man really understand the full significance of the terrible disease, aneurysm—that swelling of the great artery leading from the heart, which was liable at any second to rupture and cause instantaneous death? Was he ignorant of the fact that a few short months must see him cold in his grave?

Hyslop sighed, and a great curiosity possessed him about Hay. Indeed, when the surgery was over and the young doctor came into the dining room to supper, he was moved to make a discreet inquiry.

Cameron was out on a case, but Janet gave him the information he sought.

"Ay, indeed," she responded. "Weel do I ken Bob Hay. A sore heartbreak he's been to his folks, and a sorer heartbreak still to Chrissie Temple."

Janet paused, then severely continued: "A fine

young fella he was at ane time, mind ye. He come o' decent stock; Bob was the only son. He went to the academy an' then into the yard to serve his time for the drawin' office.

"Weel, he showed considerable promise in his wark, was likit by a' folks in the office, an' took a pleasant part in the sociability o' the toun. An' to crown a', at twenty-three he twined up wi' Chrissie Temple an' took to courtin' her serious. Maybe ye'll ken Chrissie Temple, doctor?"

Hyslop nodded, and Janet went on:

"Ay, an' a fine sweet woman she is. Though, mind ye, in thae days she was bonnier by far, a sparky dark-e'ed lass fu' o' speerits an' desperate ta'en with Bob. They were plighted, ye ken.

"Weel, in the spring o' the next year it so fell out that Bob got the offer o' a post wi' ane o' the big Indian companies out in Bombay. 'Twas a grand opportunity, which baith Chrissie and Bob agreed he couldna afford to neglect—a chance for advancement which would bring him, after five years, back to Levenford an' the yard in a braw superior poseetion.

"So Bob took his leave 'midst tears an' a' that show o' fondness, swearin' he would be true to Chrissie, as weel he micht, an' for some months a' went richt an' proper. Then Bob's letters home turned less regular, an' finally they stoppit a' thegither. Then about a year after Bob had gone, Chrissie got a letter frae the bla'guard breakin' aff the engagement.

"Weel, she was fair struck down. She said nothing,

but frae that day a change cam' ower the lass. She held hersel' awa' frae the life o' the toun.

"Weel, time went on, an' the gap between Bob Hay an' Levenford widened. Nae mair was heard of him except shamefu' stories o' his deevilries. Fair brokenhearted, Bob's mother withered awa'. An' his father was laid i' the graveyard not long after. But Chrissie still kept up her heid. Off an' on she had offers, but she refused them a'."

When Janet slipped out eventually and left Hyslop to his supper, he reflected somberly on what he had heard and felt an added loathing of this man who had come back, broken, debauched and dying, but brazen to the last.

Time went on, and Bob Hay remained in Levenford. The townspeople spurned him as they would have spurned a dog, yet Bob did not seem to care. He showed himself a great deal in public, whistling, carefree, shameless. And every month, disreputable, but irrepressible as ever, he appeared at the surgery for the certificate which entitled him to draw his pension.

On the first of September, however, Hay did not make his customary appearance, and Hyslop wondered what could have befallen the unfortunate reprobate.

He was not long in doubt. A message arrived the following day asking him to visit Hay at the Inverclyde Hotel. The doctor found him in a back room of the hotel, a disreputable tavern behind Quayside.

Hay was in bed, unshaven, pallid and apparently in

pain. Yet his demeanor was as defiant as before. "Sorry to trouble you, doctor sahib," he croaked. "Can't seem to get on the old pins today."

Hyslop sat down. "You've been drinking, I suppose," he said.

For a moment it looked as though a hot denial were on Hay's lips; then he laughed. "Why not? A bit of a scatter does a fellow good once in a while, eh, doc?"

Hyslop was shocked. He exclaimed, "In the name of God, Hay, why do you go on this way? It would be bad enough at the best of times. But don't you realize you've only a few months to live?"

"Humbug, doctor sahib!" wheezed Hay. "You go tell that to the horse marines."

"I'm telling it to you," persisted Hyslop. "Why don't you take yourself in hand?"

"Take myself in hand? Ha! Ha! That's a good one, doc! Why should I?"

"For your own sake, Hay."

There was a pause, while Hay, with unwavering defiance, met Hyslop's entreating gaze. It seemed hopeless. Hyslop was about to open his bag when a strange phenomenon arrested him.

Hay's cheek began to twitch, and a tear fell from his eye. Desperately he tried to hold his pose of indifference, but it was no use. He gave way completely and sobbed as if his heart would break.

"Don't take on, man," Hyslop muttered. "Pull yourself together."

"Pull myself together!" sobbed Hay hysterically. "That's good, that is! What do you think I've been doing ever since I came home but pull myself together? Do you think it's been nice for me, coming back like a beaten dog to die in the gutter? Haven't I tried to put a face on things? God in heaven, haven't I tried?

"You think I've been drinking, but I haven't touched a drop since I came back. Do you know what my allowance is? Three pounds a month. A fine time a man can have on that—especially a man like me, whose heart is liable to burst at any minute." And convulsed by an agony of pain and grief, Hay writhed on the bed.

There was a long silence; then Hyslop put his hand on Hay's shoulders. He had misjudged this man: what he had mistaken for cheap effrontery was merely the mask of courage.

"Cheer up!" he whispered. "We'll do something about it."

"No, it's no use. They won't own me here," Hay retorted in a voice of anguish. "Nobody speaks to me. They only want to spit at me. Oh, don't think I'm complaining. I deserve it. The sooner I'm dead, the better."

As Hay spoke, a curious expression appeared on Hyslop's face—that look which usually betokened the making of an important decision. He said no more; but rising, he walked out of the room.

About an hour later, when Hay had sobbed his

grief out, the door opened and someone came into the room. He turned his head, and a cry came from his lips.

"You!" he whispered as if in awe. "You—Chrissie!"

Slowly she came forward. She sat down beside the bed and took his hand.

He groaned: "Go away and let me be. Haven't I harmed you enough? Go away."

"But I don't want to go, Bob," she whispered. "If you'll let me, I'd rather stay. It's now that you need me."

She smiled at him, and there was that in her smile which silenced him. He bowed his head against her breast, his pain forgotten in the knowledge of her love.

Later he tried to explain haltingly his faithlessness—how he had been swept off his feet by wild companions and led into debt. She listened, compassionate and understanding, smoothing his hair.

Twilight found them thus and drew a veil over their reconciliation.

A week later Levenford was stirred by the news that Bob Hay and Chrissie Temple had married. Afterwards Bob was driven home to Chrissie's house, which stood on the top of the Lea Brae, with a small garden from which there was a lovely view of the Firth of Clyde.

Healed in mind and spirit, if not in body, Bob knew the comforting attention of a good woman.

When spring came again, Chrissie would take him into the garden, where he would sit with his hand fondly in his wife's, watching the ships sail out to the great beyond.

A strange honeymoon, but a happy one! Bob lived all through the summer in great happiness and peace, his pretense and cheap flashiness gone, meeting his pain and suffering with strength and patience.

When the first colors of autumn were creeping over the landscape and the first leaves fluttering gently from the trees, Bob Hay passed peacefully away—sailing away, like the ships, into the great beyond.

And Chrissie was there beside him when he died. She still keeps much to herself but when Hyslop sees her, it seems to him that instead of sadness, happiness is written on her face.

INHERITANCE

IT WAS a warm June afternoon and the practice had run slack—so slack, indeed, that Doctor Cameron had slipped off to Peebles for a week's holiday,

With mind and body equally at rest, Doctor Finlay Hyslop stood by the window of the front room, gazing idly toward the green of the lawn and the waving trees beyond. All at once the clang of the gate caught his ear, and turning his head, he observed young Gavin Birrell and Lucy Anderson coming up the drive.

A pleasant sight they made as they approached the house, laughing and talking, glancing at each other in loving companionship. Gavin wore flannels, while Lucy's dress was of pure white silk. Obviously they had been playing tennis. There was about them something of the freshness of the early summer day, an air of brightness and promise. Hyslop knew them only slightly, but like everyone else in town, he was aware that they were to be married next month.

Lucy was of good sound Levenford stock. She was fair and pretty, with laughing blue eyes and a certain artlessness of manner which made her a great favorite in the town. She was only nineteen.

Gavin himself was only twenty-two, a slight, sensitive-faced youngster. His father Edgar Birrell, originally a native of Dalbeith, some twenty miles from Levenford, had spent most of his life in the Argentine, where he had amassed a considerable fortune in cattle ranching.

Two years before, Edgar Birrell had returned to his native Scotland with his son—his wife was dead—and had taken one of the large houses on Knoxhill. A retired man, apparently without a care in the world, he had sought the good opinion of his neighbors by throwing himself into the public life of the town.

In a short space of time he became a member of the Town Council and chairman of the Cottage Hospital Committee. He was an elder of the Parish Church. His name figured at the head of subscription lists to popular charities. On all sides it was agreed that Edgar Birrell conferred distinction and benefit upon Levenford.

In appearance he was small and narrow-shouldered, with a mane of white hair, dark eyebrows, a sallow, slightly pitted skin and small, deep-set eyes which wore always a look of timid probity. It was a moving sight to see him leading the singing on Sundays, standing with his head thrown back, his shrill voice rising above the others.

And yet, though Doctor Hyslop knew nothing to the man's discredit, he could not look upon him without feeling that his heart harbored some secret fear. Something furtive in the glint of that deep-set eye, a stray erratic gesture quickly concealed, an undertone of sadness in that high-pitched voice made Hyslop sense a troubled conscience and a soul ill at ease. Despite Edgar Birrell's affluence and admirable reputation, he aroused in the young doctor a queer, unwilling pity.

But here the bell rang, and in a moment Janet came in to announce Mr. Gavin Birrell and his young lady. Hyslop went into the waiting room, and at the sight of the two young people he beamed upon them.

"This is pretty good of you," he declared, "taking pity on an old bachelor who's got all the worries of Levenford on his shoulders."

Birrell grinned boyishly. "As a matter of fact," he said, "we've come to add to your worries." He paused, gazing sideways at his fiancée, "It's all Lucy's doing. She's dragged me here by main force."

"That isn't very complimentary to Doctor Hyslop, Gavin," laughed Lucy.

The doctor shook his head in mock dismay. "What can you expect from a man who's going to be married next month? He's living in a perfect daze."

An odd little silence followed this innocent remark; then Gavin said, "As a matter of fact, doctor, I have felt a bit dazed lately. And this afternoon I had quite a groggy turn on the tennis court. Couldn't hit a ball, and my legs seemed all over the place, just as if I was drunk. Oh, I know it's nothing, absolutely nothing. It's ridiculous to bother you, but—well, Lucy has dragged me along. She's started bossing me already, you see."

"And high time, too," Lucy interposed lightheartedly. "I've never seen you play such tennis as you did this afternoon."

"Come into the surgery, then, and I'll put you through your paces," Hyslop said cheerfully to Gavin. "You're run down, perhaps. You may want a tonic, or something simple like that."

Lucy held out her hand to the doctor. "I'll have to go," she said. "There are some people coming for tea. Good-by, Gavin dear. Don't be too hard on him, please, Doctor Hyslop. Good-by." And smiling, she was gone.

Hyslop led the way into the consulting room.

"It's too bad to waste your time like this, doctor," Gavin began apologetically. "It was just a turn I took this afternoon. I've had them before—not quite so noticeable, perhaps, but I don't attach the slightest importance to them."

"What kind of turn?" asked Hyslop.

"Oh, just as I told you," answered Gavin with a half-laugh. "I seem to come over groggy, as if my legs and arms didn't belong to me. I've no power in my limbs."

"There's an easy way of setting your mind at rest,"

said Hyslop, "We call it Romberg's test. Suppose you stand out in the middle of the floor. That's right. Hands by your sides, feet together, head up. Now close your eyes."

Gavin, standing erect and unsupported in the center of the floor, closed his eyes, and immediately swayed like a reed in the wind. Every second he threatened to fall flat upon his face, and soon, with a little gasp, he opened his eyes and clutched at the wall for support.

"There!" he exclaimed, smiling rather doubtfully. "That's exactly how it takes me."

But there was no answering smile on Doctor Hyslop's face. A look of consternation flashed over his features. Taking Gavin's wrist, he drew him to the window. In the strong light, he examined his eyes carefully. Then he said, "Sit down in this chair a moment and cross your legs."

Gavin sat down, and taking a small rubber-capped hammer, Hyslop tapped each knee sharply. There was no answering jerk. The reflex was dead.

"What's all this fuss about, doctor?" protested Gavin.

At first Hyslop did not answer. Then he said, "Seeing you've taken the trouble to come in, Gavin, I want you to let me have a real good look at you."

Gavin gazed at the doctor in amazement, but there was something in the latter's tone which compelled obedience. The young man slowly peeled off his flannels.

Then, with an impassive face, Hyslop made a complete examination. He examined Gavin's hands. He examined the reaction and condition of his muscles. For a full fifteen minutes, using the ophthalmoscope this time, he examined his eyes, and finally, asking Gavin to repeat certain difficult words, he made a close investigation of his speech.

When at last he had finished, he put away his instruments and sat down at his desk, his eyes fixed upon the blotter in front of him.

A long time he sat like this. At length he lifted his eyes and looked straight at young Birrell. Yet he did not see Gavin's face. He saw the face of old Edgar Birrell, smooth, rather sallow, topped by the noble mane of pure white hair.

He saw, too, by the power of his imagination, the faces and the figures of other Birrells, reaching back in the family line. And a crooked, palsied line it was . . .

"You are an only son?" Hyslop asked.

"Why, yes." Gavin flushed, as he did so easily. "I had two brothers, I believe, but they both died when they were little."

There was a long pause; then Hyslop demanded in the same constrained fashion, "Your father—do you know anything of his family? Has he any living relatives?"

Gavin's high color persisted. "No," he answered. "I don't know much about my father's folks. He never speaks of them. But really, I don't see what all this has to do with me."

"It has a great deal to do with you, I'm afraid."

"Afraid? In the name of heaven, what's all this mystery, doctor? You're looking at me very strangely." His cheek began to twitch. "I wish you'd come to the point."

Remembering Gavin's impending marriage, Hyslop was swept by a great wave of pitying compunction. He could not think what to say, or how to say it. He felt the utter impossibility of telling the truth, and yet he had to. There was no other way.

"I want to come to the point," he muttered. "But it's not easy, Gavin. You see, I'm afraid this isn't quite so slight as you imagine. It isn't just that you're run down. You've got ataxia, Gavin, a rare, hereditary form, not unlike Friedreich's.

"Oh, I don't want to worry you with long-sounding names or technicalities, but the plain truth is that we're up against something pretty desperate. I'll have to ask you to see a specialist."

"A specialist!" gasped Birrell. "You can't be serious! I haven't time to see him. I have to go up to Tannochbrae tomorrow, to see about the cottage for our honeymoon. Hang it all, doctor, remember I'm being married next month."

"I think it might be as well, Gavin," Hyslop said in a low voice, "if you made up your mind—to postpone your wedding."

"Postpone my wedding!" exclaimed Birrell. "But it's all arranged! Everything! And there's nothing the matter with me. Oh, why do you look at me like that? I've done nothing wrong."

Hyslop kept his eyes steadily upon the young man, "Gavin," he said, "you're right. It's nothing you've done. But you're paying for it just the same."

A long pause. Then: "It's your inheritance, Gavin. You know that certain conditions are hereditary. Well, this is one of them. We don't know what causes it. Nobody's to blame for it. We only know it as a family disease—terrible, obscure, incurable. Down it comes from one generation to another, skipping one person, perhaps, in every four, but ravaging the others like an insidious plague.

"I've no doubt your two brothers died of it. I've no doubt, if you looked back into your father's antecedents, you'd find a dark and pitiful story. Though he escaped, he should never have married, for he's transmitted the scourge to you. As for you, Gavin—you haven't escaped."

Slowly the terrible meaning of the doctor's words dawned upon Gavin. A violent spasm of denial shook him.

"No!" he cried. "I don't believe you! I'll go and see somebody else."

"That's what I suggest," Hyslop said gently. "You must let me send you to the specialist. He'll advise you."

"I don't want advice!" cried Gavin. "I only want to prove you're wrong."

"So long as you go to him," said Hyslop quietly,

taking up his pen, "I don't mind what you think of me. Wait, Gavin, and I'll give you a letter for him now."

Gavin said no more, but he waited, ashen pale with resentment and anger, until the doctor had finished writing; then without a word he took the letter.

Hyslop rose and put his arm soothingly across Birrell's shoulders, but with a broken sob the young man pushed him away. "Let me be!" he cried, trembling violently. "I'll have nothing more to do with you." And abruptly he left the house.

All the next day Finlay Hyslop went drearily about his work, harassed and oppressed by the predicament in which young Birrell was so innocently involved.

The day passed slowly. Hyslop got through his cases as expeditiously as he could, finished his evening surgery, and then sat waiting, hoping against hope that Gavin would call to see him.

At last, toward eleven o'clock, the doorbell rang. Hyslop hurried to the door himself and opened it.

Gavin stood there. Although his face was pale, his voice was quiet and controlled. "I'm sorry to be so late," he said. "One or two things have kept me."

He followed the doctor into the sitting room in a curious tranquility. All emotion seemed to have been driven out of him.

"I want to apologize," he remarked. "I behaved very badly yesterday. You see, it was a shock to me." A pause. "You were right, of course, in everything you said."

Another pause, then Hyslop muttered, "I wish to God I had been wrong!"

"The specialist was extremely kind," Birrell went on. "He confirmed your opinion. There's no doubt at all. I made him tell me everything." The calm, impersonal voice broke suddenly, revealing a depth of tortured bitterness. "So I know what to look forward to. These giddy attacks will get more frequent. Soon I'll begin to stagger all over the place. In a year or two I won't be able to walk at all. My eyesight will suffer and my speech may go.

"Oh, yes, I know all about it. I forced him to give me the whole story clear. So there I'll lie, so help me, God, paralyzed and incurable—helpless until I die. A pretty picture of a bridegroom, doctor."

"It's cruel," Hyslop muttered. "And you not a bit to blame."

"No one is to blame," said Gavin quickly. "Not my father, if that's what you mean. Let me tell you what I did, doctor, after I'd seen the specialist. I took the train to Dalbeith—that's why I'm so late—and I went through the parish register there. It's just what you suspected—the history of the Birrells is pretty tragic.

"But my father—don't you see how he must have felt? He knew he'd missed the cursed thing; he wanted to get married, and he took his chance. Oh, I don't blame him, doctor. But oh, God, what a muddle it is now between poor Lucy and me!"

"I've been trying to think things out for you,

Gavin," Doctor Hyslop said. "It's hard, I know, but wouldn't it be better if you went away from Levenford for a bit, just cut everything sudden and clean, without waiting for all the outcry and the sympathy and the hateful notoriety?"

Gavin looked across at him with a twisted face. "The specialist wanted me to go to a nerve home up in the hills."

"Yes, that's right, Gavin," said Hyslop.

"And wait there, I suppose, until they carry me out on a stretcher?"

"No, no," cut in the doctor imploringly. "You mustn't talk that way, man. We've got to face this thing."

There was a silence. Gavin sighed. His tranquility returned.

"You're right," he said. "We've got to face it. There's no use making a fuss. Besides, there's Lucy to think of; we must do things so that they turn out best for her." He smiled at Hyslop. "You've been very patient and kind. I'm afraid I've not appeared too grateful."

"You're going to take my advice?" asked the doctor anxiously.

"Yes." Gavin nodded slowly. "I'll get out of Levenford. I'm sure it's best."

"Come in here tomorrow and we can make all the arrangements," insisted Hyslop. "I'll do everything . . . But it's going to be horrible for you to tell Lucy."

"I shan't tell her just yet," said Gavin, without

visible emotion. "I have one or two things I must do first. Arrangements to make and unmake. For instance, I must go and settle about the cottage."

He smiled at Hyslop with a new courage. "You knew we'd arranged to spend a month there, at Tannochbrae. But now I'll have to cancel it. I'll go at the end of the week. And then Lucy must be told."

At this he rose abruptly, as though the thought pierced him beyond the limits of his stoic endurance. He held out his hand to Hyslop, thanked him once again, and left the house.

Hyslop went sadly upstairs to his room. Gavin's quiet fortitude under this crushing blow served only to increase the sorrow in the doctor's heart.

As the week passed, Hyslop longed for Cameron's return in order that he might unburden himself of the whole story.

On Saturday, toward four in the afternoon, while Hyslop was at tea, Cameron arrived. The old doctor entered quickly, in a state of great excitement. He offered no greetings. An early edition of the evening paper was in his hand.

"Have you seen what's happened? It's terrible, isn't it? Poor lad!"

"What are you talking about?" asked Hyslop in perplexity.

"There's been a terrible accident up on the loch. Young Gavin Birrell went up there to see that the cottage was ready for his honeymoon. He went out just for an hour to try a cast. The boat was capsized. He was drowned."

A long and heavy silence filled the room. Hyslop could not speak. Now he understood Gavin's ready acquiescence—the best, the only remedy . . .

The tragedy made a profound sensation in Levenford. Everybody was horrified by the calamity almost on the eve of Gavin's marriage.

After the first intolerable shock, Lucy bore up nobly. She had sweet and lovely memories to sustain her. No one dreamed of the real facts of the case. There was no scandal, no malicious gossip in the town, only sympathy and regret.

At the funeral, the cortege stretched for a quarter of a mile down the narrow streets and the church was more densely crowded than it would have been for the wedding that had so gaily been planned.

Finlay Hyslop went, too, and was swept by the slow crowds into a seat from which he had a full view of the bereaved father.

He gazed in fascination at the thin and sallow face under its crown of snowy hair. At that moment Edgar Birrell turned and met his eyes.

As Hyslop stared at those lined and tragic features, a flash of understanding passed between the two men. And it came to the young doctor, with a great pity, that out of all those present, another knew besides himself.

NIGHT CALL

IT WAS a wet and dark December night. The wind howled down the narrow valley among the scattered houses of Levenford, driving the rain against the windowpanes and scouring the streets.

It had been a grueling day for Doctor Finlay Hyslop. When he finished his last round he came in, soaked to the skin, mentally fagged, tired as a beaten dog.

He flung himself into bed, bone-weary, praying that he would not be disturbed, and fell into a heavy sleep.

The faint whirring of a bell half awakened him. Still dazed with sleep, he took up the receiver of the telephone beside his bed.

A woman's voice spoke instantly, but from far away. "Come at once, doctor. Come to Robert Glen's farm by Yarrow."

Finlay Hyslop groaned. Yarrow was a good five

miles away, among the mountains. "I can't get up to Yarrew tonight."

"But you must come tonight, doctor."

"Who are you?"

"I am Robert Glen's wife. And my daughter is very bad."

"I'll come in the morning."

"Oh, no. For God's sake, doctor, you must come now!"

Finlay Hyslop could have sworn aloud, but the pitiful urgency of the voice persuaded him. He dropped the receiver, rose, tumbled into his damp clothes and picked up his bag.

Outside, the rain had ceased but the wind was bitterly cold. He harnessed the dogcart hurriedly . . .

After a journey which seemed unending, he reached the lonely house. Large and rambling, surrounded by stunted birches, it was a gloomy and dilapidated barracks. Not a glimmer of light was visible as he trudged up the narrow path between the trees, and only the remote hooting of an owl broke the stillness.

He pulled the bell. There was no answer. He stood for a moment listening, hearing nothing but that distant, mocking owl. Then, with angry impatience, he battered against the heavy door with his foot.

Immediately there arose the furious barking of dogs, and after a long delay the door was opened by an oldish woman in a dingy black dress and shawl. She peered at Hyslop with a frightened, hooded face that seemed, by the lantern she held, as heavy and pale as a bladder of lard. Two hounds growled at her heels.

Furious at such a churlish reception, Hyslop pushed past her into a large stone-flagged room, barely furnished and badly lighted, that seemed half kitchen and half parlor. Here his eyes fell at once upon a young girl who lay wrapped in blankets upon a horsehair sofa beside the fire. She seemed to be in a state of coma.

Beside her, in an attitude of watchfulness, sat a powerful, thickset man. Six feet six he must have stood when his massive frame was erect, and he had enormous shoulders like a bull's.

He was in his shirt sleeves, wore rough gray knickerbockers and no shoes, and his air of general disorder was made more uncouth by a tangled mane of iron-gray hair. He might have been fifty-five years of age. He was Robert Glen, without a doubt.

So intent was his scrutiny of the unconscious girl he did not hear Hyslop enter, but as the doctor heaved his bag upon the table the man swung round, his eyes burning in his dark face with such wildness that the doctor was taken aback.

"What do you want?" Glen demanded.

"I'm the doctor," Hyslop answered. "If you'll step aside, I'll have a look at the patient. She looks pretty bad."

"Doctor!" The blood flooded Robert Glen's brow. "I won't have doctors here. Get out! D'ye hear me?

Get out!"

Glen's manner was formidable, but a sense of indignation sustained the doctor. He thought of his weary drive through the wintry darkness, and he resented this boorish treatment at the end of it. He said hotly, "You're crazy to talk like that. That girl is gravely ill. In the name of heaven, let me try to help her."

"I don't trust doctors," Glen muttered.

Hyslop glanced toward the woman who stood in mortal terror by the doorway, her hands clasped on her breast. He presumed that she had shot her bolt in summoning him against her lord and master's will. No further help could be expected there. Only one course seemed likely to succeed.

Hyslop moved to the table and picked up his bag. "Very well. If your daughter dies, you know who is responsible."

For a moment Robert Glen was silent, his eyes filled with the conflict between his hatred and his fear.

Hyslop's hand was almost on the door when Glen cried, "Don't go! If she's bad like ye say, ye'd better look at her."

The doctor came back to the sofa, knelt down and examined the patient. She was about eighteen years old, and there was in her slender immaturity a strange, uncared-for beauty.

She moaned when Hyslop moved her gently. Her skin was burning to the touch. He was puzzled as to the cause of the infection until he saw the swelling behind her left ear—acute suppurative mastoiditis. Hyslop's heart sank.

When he had made quite sure, he turned to Glen. "This is desperately serious. You ought to have sent for me days ago."

"It's only inflammation," Glen muttered. "We've used goose grease and bran poultices. I'm fetching leeches tomorrow from the loch. She will be better then."

"She will be dead then."

Robert Glen stood before Hyslop like a man paralyzed.

"Look here, Glen." The doctor spoke vehemently. "There's an abscess in this left mastoid bone. Unless it's drained, it will break through the skull into the brain. Unless we do something at once, your daughter has about six hours to live."

The other man reached out to the wall as if for support. "Is that the truth?"

"What earthly reason have I for lying?"

Glen's jaw clenched. "Do it, then. She maun get better."

A thrill of apprehension shot through Hyslop. He had persuaded Glen to let him operate. What would happen if he failed?

He opened his bag, laid out instruments and dressings, prepared two basins of carbolic solution. Then, between them, the two men lifted the patient onto the bare wooden table. Hyslop placed the mask saturated with ether over her face.

Four minutes later he summoned all his courage and picked up a lancet from the tray. The light, a flaring oil lamp held by Glen, was atrocious, the conditions unimaginably bad; the operation, even under the most favorable circumstances, was both delicate and dangerous.

Though in hospital Doctor Hyslop had done a fair amount of routine work, he knew himself as an indifferent surgeon. And now he realized that he had to make only one tiny slip, and he was through—fatally through into the lateral sinus of the brain.

All that he had seen the great Macewen do so skillfully, all that he had read in textbooks, evaded him in this moment of need. He worked by instinct, feeling his way blindly, conscious that the wild eyes of Robert Glen were upon him . . .

He was down to the bone now, the delicate bone of the skull. With a small gouge he cut into the antrum. The bone offered more resistance than he had expected. Was there no focus, after all? Had he made some fatal error of judgment?

A cold sweat broke over him. Slowly, but with increasing despair, he went deeper and deeper still. And then, when he felt he must surely pierce into the brain itself, he reached the seat of the trouble.

He carefully scraped the cavity, washed it with antiseptic, packed it with iodoform gauze. Five more minutes and the patient was back upon her improvised bed, breathing quietly and deeply, as if asleep.

For a full hour Hyslop did not leave her side. Twice he took her temperature. In that short space it fell a full point and a half. Her pulse was stronger, too. He was convinced that she would recover.

He got up at last and packed his bag, filled with that sense of achievement which comes on rare occasions to the long-suffering general practitioner. All this time he had neither glanced at Robert Glen nor spoken to him, but now he threw a look at him.

The man stood by the table where, during the past hour, he had remained immobile, watching Hyslop.

The doctor, noting that the sullenness was gone from Glen's dark face, said with grim triumph, "She'll do now."

The other man stammered, "Y-yes, indeed, she—she does look better."

Finlay Hyslop could see that Glen was swept by a terrible emotion—torn between gratitude and that rooted hatred and distrust of his fellowmen. The doctor's anger died and he felt a rush of pity. This man was so transparently affected by the prospect of his daughter's recovery.

To ease the situation, Hyslop nodded toward the woman of the house, who had slipped toward the bed to take the place he had vacated. "One thing you mustn't forget. We owe thanks to your wife for asking me to come."

Glen's somber eyes followed the doctor's in bewilderment. "I do not understand," he muttered. "That is Jeanie, our servant. She can't speak English—only Gaelic."

"But man alive!" Hyslop expostulated. "Don't you know that's how I got the call? She telephoned me to come here."

Robert Glen gazed at him wonderingly. "There is no telephone for miles."

One glance at Glen's eyes convinced the doctor that he spoke the truth. He faced Glen dizzily. He gasped, "Good God, man, don't you realize that your wife begged me to make this call? Telephone or no telephone, she spoke to me this very night. I asked her who she was and she told me plainly that she was your wife."

Towering above the doctor, Robert Glen raised his clenched fist passionately. Hyslop thought the man was about to fell him. Then, with a great effort, Glen mastered himself. He said hoarsely, "My wife died in this room five years ago."

THE THIRD INGREDIENT

THE discussion following the divisional meeting of the Medical Association was being held in the rooms of the Philosophical Society in Levenford. Doctor Finlay Hyslop and his partner, Doctor Cameron, were there in company with all the doctors of the town and the surrounding country.

Supper had been partaken of and now talk was in full swing, but the pleasant debate was being ruined by an ass. Doctor Snoddie was airing his supercilious views on—the fallacy of the bottle of medicine!

"Surely, the basis of medical treatment is science—pure science," he declared. "In these modern days you can't expect to get results by the antiquated expedient of a bottle of physic."

There was a nasty pause—most of the company had been busy prescribing bottles of physic that very day. Suddenly old Doctor Cameron spoke.

"Perhaps yes," he said; "perhaps no. And perhaps

some of us dunderheads use ingredients in our prescriptions that you scientific men don't recognize!"

"I beg your pardon," said Snoddie.

"Well," answered Cameron, "I'm thinking of one particular ingredient—yes, and one particular case."

I don't deal in duchesses in my practice (Cameron continued in his own dry style). Nor in dukes, either. And Jamie was only a barber's assistant when first I knew him. A little fellow, dark and active and obliging. That was Jamie until the war came along. Jamie volunteered and was rejected because he was too small. In the end, he went with me in the R.A.M.C. When the war was over, he came back and put his gratuity into a barber's business opposite my surgery.

He was the same as before the war: shy, mild, trustworthy and timid—oh, timid as a tube of his own toothpaste. He sold this as a sideline—he was so taken up with his shop, so eager to get on.

It was this same toothpaste that introduced him to Nancy, who dropped into his shop one night on her way home from work. Nancy was a pretty girl, with laughing eyes and a teasing tilt to her head.

Jamie was stricken by the thunderbolt. After that his business took second place in the constellations of the universe. A brighter star had swum into the horizon. Its name was Nancy.

Then one evening three months later, Jamie came into my surgery looking as if he had lost that star.

"Why, what's the matter, Jamie?" I asked. "Has

she refused you?"

"Refused me!" blurted out Jamie. "No, no, doctor. I can't—I couldn't—I haven't given her the chance. I can't ask her. I haven't the nerve. I'm nothing, and she's so beautiful."

"Don't you want her, you idiot?"

"Oh!" gasped Jamie.

"Ask her, then, and be done with it."

"I can't, sir," he almost moaned. "I—I've tried everything. I've even tried to stiffen myself up with whisky. No use! It only made me stupid. That's why I've come to you, doctor. Give me something, please, to—to tone up my nerve. I know you can!"

I gave Jamie a queer look. "Have you been hearing about something—some drug I've got here?"

"You've got something, then?" he cried. "For heaven's sake, give me a dose!"

"Well, Jamie," I said with extreme hesitation, "I *have* got something here, but if it was known I—"

"I'll not tell a soul, doctor!"

"Thirty drops of it, Jamie, and you'd knock down a prizefighter."

"That's—that's what I'm needing."

I went into the dispensary and mixed him a draft. I came back and handed him the glass.

"Take it, Jamie. Then get the job over quick, man, before the effect wears off."

Jamie gulped the dose, snatched up his hat and tore out of the room.

It was nine before I closed up to go home. On the

way to my house I ran into Jamie. He began to stammer his thanks.

"Did you ask Nancy, then?" I asked.

"Ask her!" he shouted. "With that marvelous stuff in me, I didn't wait to ask her. I walked straight up to her and hugged her till she said yes. We're to be married next month."

Well, Nancy became Mrs. Jamie amid a great shower of confetti and stale jokes.

The marriage was a great success. The realities were there: I saw the three of them into the world myself—all boys.

Five years passed, and Jamie had no reason to regret that drug I had so rashly used. Then I began to notice things across the way. Chiefly Jamie. All at once his smile slipped off; his face dulled. But Nancy sparkled more than ever—a hard sparkle through which there gleamed a sort of sullen contempt.

One day I tackled Jamie. "What the devil has come over you?" I asked.

"It's Macintosh—and Nancy!"

"Why let a lout like that hang about your house?" I said sharply.

"Nancy likes to have him to drop in."

"Kick him out," I said, more sharply.

I knew Macintosh—half loafer, half bruiser; flashy, sporty, loud-voiced.

"Yes, I'll—I'll have to see about it," stammered Jamie in the old timid way.

Several days passed. Jamie was moodier, Nancy

harder—a silly woman touched in her stupid vanity. Then, at the end of the week, Jamie flung into the surgery.

"I can't put up with it. In my own house! To think I've got to sit and watch that big brute making eyes at my wife!"

"You know the remedy," I said coldly.

"I can't do it!" he cried miserably. "It's impossible. You know he could lay me out with one punch." Suddenly he stiffened. "Doctor!" he gasped. "I was forgetting. That stuff you gave me before. You said—and by heaven, it *did* make me feel fit to lay out a prizefighter."

"No, no," I said hurriedly. "I'm not going to risk that again."

If I said no once, I said it twenty times; but there was no getting away from Jamie's pleading. Despite my fear of the consequences, I found myself mixing the same dose I had given him before.

"It's stronger this time, Jamie," I said.

He tossed it down and started across the street. I was doubtful this time as to the efficacy of the potion, so I followed him—slipped into the house behind him.

From the hall I had a clear view: Nancy on one side of the fire, Macintosh on the other, each with a glass of beer at hand.

"Oh, it's yoursel', Jamie," said Nancy, looking up with tolerant contempt. "Run over like a guid lad and buy us a paper."

Jamie took no notice. He was shaking, but I could see his hands clench. "Get out of my house, Macintosh," he said.

"Ah, don't be botherin' me, Jamie," said Macintosh.

"Get out, will you!" shouted Jamie.

Macintosh winked at Nancy. "Do you hear him now?"

"For the last time," fired out Jamie, "will you go?"

In answer, Macintosh tilted back the legs of his chair, balanced himself with easy arrogance. But he balanced for only a second. Jamie smashed his fist full into Macintosh's grinning face. With a crash, over went Macintosh onto the fender.

"So that's it!" snarled Macintosh, getting to his feet. A smear of red was on his cheek from a cut above his eye. "You think you can lick me, you little squirt?"

He rushed at Jamie, but Jamie didn't wait. He tore into Macintosh like a wild cat gone mad. I never saw anything like it. Jamie knew no more about boxing than his own shaving brush. Swinging his arms widely, he hit Macintosh chiefly in the stomach, and that was bad for Macintosh.

Jamie butted Macintosh; he stuck to him, clawing; he wound himself round Macintosh's legs. Macintosh cursed, panted, struggled. They fell on the floor—Jamie on top. The sound of Macintosh's head on that hard floor was like a mallet on an empty barrel—a lovely crash!

Macintosh's eyes went glassy. He was out. The next moment Jamie was across his chest punching Macintosh's nose.

I ran in. "Don't! I cried, dragging Jamie off. "You'll spoil him for life."

"I want to!" shouted Jamie.

For a minute Macintosh lay on his back—a wreck! Then he staggered to his feet.

"Get out of my house," roared Jamie, "before I kick you out!"

Macintosh went out in a hurry. With a cry of rapture, Nancy ran forward.

"Jamie," she cried, flinging her arms around him, "I didn't know you could! Oh, Jamie, you're wonderful!"

"That's right, Nancy," said Jamie coolly. "Remember, I'm boss in this house in the future. Run into the shop like a guid lass and fetch some plaster for my eye."

"Yes, Jamie," said Nancy meekly.

Jamie came with me to the door. One eye was closed, but the other glowed with happiness. "I don't know how to thank you," he said. "I don't know what you gave me, but it was grand stuff."

Then I told Jamie what I'd given him.

When old Cameron had finished there was a murmur of curiosity.

"Well," said Doctor Snoddie with a sneer, "what *did* you use? Maximum dose of strychnine?"

"I used three things," said Cameron, knocking the ashes from his pipe. "The first was water. The second was a drop or two of burnt sugar to color the water."

"And the third?" shouted half a dozen of the company.

"The third was the ingredient I spoke about. I often use it." Old Cameron grinned and added, *"It was just faith."*

CPSIA information can be obtained
at www.ICGtesting.com
Printed in the USA
BVHW040911230120
570296BV00014B/468